Sinfully Summer

AIMEE DUFFY

Harper*Impulse* an imprint of
HarperCollins*Publishers Ltd*
77–85 Fulham Palace Road
Hammersmith, London W6 8JB

www.harpercollins.co.uk

A Paperback Original 2013

First published in Great Britain in ebook format by HarperImpulse 2013

Cover Images © Shutterstock.com

Aimee Duffy asserts the moral right to
be identified as the author of this work

A catalogue record for this book
is available from the British Library

ISBN: 978-0-00-755968-8

This novel is entirely a work of fiction.
The names, characters and incidents portrayed in it are
the work of the author's imagination. Any resemblance to
actual persons, living or dead, events or localities is
entirely coincidental.

Automatically produced by Atomik ePublisher from Easypress

Chapter One

Alexa Green poked her head out of the hotel room door. She darted a glance left, then right and exhaled when she saw the corridor was empty.

'One lap,' she threw over her shoulder to her best friends, Sarah and Jenna. 'And don't you dare think about locking this door.'

If she was lucky, she guestimated she'd get all the way around her floor without seeing a soul. Nice underwear or not, getting caught in her knickers running down the halls of the most exclusive hotel in Marbella was sure to paint her cheeks pink for the first time ever. With shaky hands and a jittering belly, she took a step into the hallway. Out of all the crazy things she'd done, this topped them all. A muffled thump sounded from along the corridor and she hesitated.

'Chickening out, Lex?' Jenna asked.

Alexa gritted her teeth at the god-awful nickname. She swore they only used it to wind her up. 'Not a chance.'

Tiny gymnasts in her stomach flipped and twirled, contradicting her cool façade. She stepped further into the hall. Adrenaline ripped through her body, making her heart pound hard against her chest. She felt alive, alert and exposed in a way that was more thrilling than terrifying. She turned back to her friends, a huge smile on her face. 'See ya in a few.'

The marble floor felt cool on her bare feet as she bolted down the light, airy hall. Doors leading to other suites whirred by in a flash as she pushed herself faster; elation and a sense of freedom making her laugh breathlessly. She couldn't deny the craziness of the dare, this was one of the wildest things she'd ever done, but she couldn't say that she wasn't enjoying the thrill.

She reached the end of the long corridor and made to turn left just as the main lift doors opened and two men stepped out. Her heart stopped and, for the beat of a second, time seemed to freeze.

Oh God.

She turned and scampered in the opposite direction – away from the English rock star and his publicist. She recognised them from more than a few wild parties back in London.

There were no doors down this strip of the hotel and she wondered where on earth she was running to, but the sound of two wolf-whistles kept her feet moving.

If she was the kind of girl to blush, she'd have been scarlet from head to toe.

Panting, she reached the end of the corridor and sprinted down the hall to her right. She couldn't hear the men's footsteps over the blood pounding in her ears, so couldn't be sure if they'd followed. But she *was* sure that she wasn't going to give anyone the opportunity to perv on her up close. What kind of idiots *wolf-whistled* in this day and age?

Shiny brushed steel doors came into sight at the end of the corridor. When she reached the lift, she paused in front of it. Alexa didn't think it could be the main one, not so far away from the rooms.

She stabbed her finger into the button furiously until the doors slid open. After darting inside, she spun around, scanned the control panel then hit the 'door close' button. As the metal slid shut, she exhaled the huge breath she'd been holding.

She let out a giggle. The elevator jarred and then promptly began to move. Up. She stopped giggling and scanned the control panel, hoping a floor between where she was now and the penthouse would magically appear. It didn't.

Jenna and Sarah had booked the plushest suite for their girly holiday and that had been the top floor, just below the penthouse with a bird's eye view of the beach.

With her heart bursting out her chest and her hands shaking worse than the vibration plates at her gym, Alexa reasoned it might have been a maid who pressed the button so there was no need to panic, yet. After all, hotel managers still needed their suites cleaned. Her father had long since moved out of the penthouse of his own luxury resort but she knew from catching quick glances of the hotel mogul's adopted son, Enrique Castillo, around the hotel that he stayed here. She couldn't imagine the hunky man with the expensive tailored suits and Italian shoes would stay anywhere else. Unless he had a huge mansion on the beach, just like his parents did. Their beautiful properties were often featured on the news for hosting charity functions.

The fact that it was past six in the evening made her feel silly for praying it was a maid, but with panic threatening to render her incoherent, she had to keep a hold of her marbles and find a way out of this mess. Surely if the infamous Mr Castillo caught her, he'd chuck her and her friends out of his hotel. Ice laced the blood in her veins as trepidation washed through her.

Not to mention the paparazzi would have a field day with the story. She'd be Alexa Green, the wild-child streaker who'd gotten herself thrown out of another classy establishment. She shuddered. No way was she going to let her last single girlie holiday with her best friends end that way.

Alexa's mind whirred as she thought of a way out of it. Given the choice, she'd rather face the idiot whistlers than this. The lift ddered to a halt and she edged to the back. Her bottom met old metal, but it did nothing to cool the heated blood pounding through her veins. Watching the doors slide open, she felt the ones behind her do the same. For a brief second, she froze as two male voices bid each other goodbye in Spanish. They weren't in sight yet, so she slipped out the opposite side of the elevator and darted around the wall.

Trying to calm her breathing, Alexa took stock of her surroundings. With her heart galloping faster than a race horse, she noted that she wasn't in an entrance hall as she'd originally expected. Nope. She'd walked straight into the Castillo penthouse. The thump of metal signalled the doors closing. She held her breath.

The slap of shoes hitting the cold, granite floor had dread knotting her stomach. Mr Castillo hadn't left. Alexa struggled to breathe evenly. If he was here, calling the elevator back up would make enough noise to alert him to her presence. But that couldn't be the only way out.

If she was right, no one would rely solely on one escape route in a hotel this grand, not with the risk of fires and electrical failure. Safety officers wouldn't allow it. There must be a stairwell leading out, she just had to find it and slip away unnoticed.

The sound of the footsteps drifted away, followed by the click of a door closing. Adrenaline roared through her veins. This was her only chance. Pushing away from the wall, she rounded the lift, desperately seeking an escape. She barely noticed the plush furnishings, soft-looking leather sofas and floor to ceiling window which showcased the most spectacular view she'd ever seen. Instead she focused on the walls surrounding the elevator.

'Are you lost?'

The heavily accented voice froze her to the spot. She darted a glance toward the sound. Dark brows furrowed over the richest coloured eyes she'd seen. His gaze swept over the length of her body, then up, lingering on her rear for a beat too long. Her skin tingled under his scrutiny.

Turning her whole body to face him, she slapped a hand on her hip. 'Had a good enough look?'

His lips quirked in a sexy, lopsided grin. The jitters were back and Alexa swore the temperature in the room shot up ten degrees. Her gaze dropped to his broad shoulders, covered in a thin white t-shirt, then down to a well filled chest. She could see a dark pattern beneath the t-shirt. She longed to find out what kind of tattoo he had. Usually, tats didn't do it for her. But on that body...

'I could ask you the same thing.'

She snapped her attention back to his face. He stepped toward her, his jaw set, his eyes dancing with humour and something darker...something that made her blood heat and her mouth water.

Alexa raised her arm, palm out. 'Hold it there, Mr. Any closer and I'll scream.'

He paused by the sofa. Propping his hip against the cream leather, he folded his arms across his chest, causing the muscles to bulge. The moisture drained from her mouth and flooded in her belly.

'No one's here to hear you.' He cocked a brow. 'You seem to be forgetting where you are and,' his gaze dipped down to her breasts causing the nipples to peak against the lacy fabric 'how underdressed.'

Alexa thought this moment would have topped the blush scale. She planted her other hand on her hip and glared at him, unwilling to show any weakness. 'I'm just leaving.'

She turned and strode back to the lift, keeping her back straight and trying not to wiggle her hips too much. The predatory sheen in his eyes made her body more jittery than the idea of sprinting around the lower floor in her underwear. She reached out to hit the button, but a large hand circled her wrist before she made it.

Alexa squeaked and darted back a step. He was so close, and his chest was *right in her face*. She could see the dark outline of the tattoo beneath the thin cotton. The outline of a burning sun, she thought, or something that looked like a sun. Her hands itched to lift the material and see for herself.

'I'm up here.'

She snapped her gaze back up to his smirking face and took another step back. His lips kicked up at the corners and his eyes darkened. She swallowed against the urge to step closer, to feel his hard body pressed against hers. But she realised she was in little more than her bra and knickers in a stranger's home. Unease skittered down her spine.

Alexa squared her shoulders, trying to quash the fear turning her heated blood into cold sludge. 'I'm leaving now.'

'After you explain what you're doing in my home in your undergarments.'

'*Undergarments?*' Alexa pressed her lips together to keep a giggle at bay. 'Seriously?'

The amusement in her eyes brought out Ric's smile—something he hadn't done in a long time. What was it about the young heiress that fascinated him? He couldn't deny that she was incredibly beautiful. A brown, messy bob fell to her shoulders and she had the greyest eyes he'd ever seen. Her lips were the perfect bow; pink, rosy and ready to be kissed. Not to mention the fact she had a body that would melt weaker men into a puddle, and he'd never seen as much of it as he had tonight.

'How do you refer to them where you're from?' he asked, knowing full well. Becoming fluent in English was the first thing he did when he left behind his former life on the streets, but he was curious to see where the conversation would go.

She cocked a perfectly manicured brow. 'You're going to ask

me what I call my underwear?' Shaking her head, she eyed the lift door over his shoulders. 'My friends will be worried.'

Disappointment pulsed through him. He didn't want her to leave. He hadn't had the time to enjoy a woman's company in so long, not since he started organising this charity ball, not to mention negotiating new contracts for the resort his adopted parents were having built at the other side of the city. Lately, all he did was work and sleep. It was the only way he was going to convince Antonio and Maria that he had changed, that they could trust him to run more than just the hotel, that he was ready to own a stake in their empire. A famous heiress showing up in his suite was most certainly a welcome distraction.

'Are you going to tell me why you're here or would you prefer to explain yourself to the police?'

She gasped and her mouth dropped open. 'You can't do that!'

Ric forced back a smile. 'And why is that? Breaking and entering is against the law.'

'Don't you know who I am?' she demanded. 'The press would *love* to snap me being carted out of a fancy hotel in my knickers.'

Her eyes pleaded with him to understand, and he did. She was in the international news on a regular basis for her wild stunts and excessive partying. A road he'd almost gone down himself, even after the Castillos had saved him.

He eyed her again, wiping all signs of recognition from his expression. Her arms folded across her chest causing the swell of her breasts to almost spill out over the white lace. Heat arrowed down to his groin and he had the urge to take a step closer. To inhale the flowery scent he'd caught a whiff of when she'd been so close before. Her eyes couldn't mask her irritation as she glared at him.

'I don't believe I do,' he lied to see how she'd react.

Her feistiness intrigued him. Given the Castillos' wealth and status, women never dared stand up to him.

'I'm Alexa Green.' She glared at him, one delicate eyebrow raised, waiting for his reaction.

Ric fought back a grin and kept his expression blank. 'That doesn't answer my question. What are you doing here?'

She dropped her arms to her sides, her fists clenched. He pressed his lips together to keep from laughing.

'A dare.'

Ric frowned. 'What?'

Alexa shook her head and huffed out a breath. 'A dare, like a bet or a—'

'I know what a dare is, Alexa. You were dared to break into my suite?'

Teasing forgotten, he eyed her again. He could have sworn she was in her twenties, younger than he, but not a minor. The last picture of her splashed over the Spanish news was of her falling out of an exclusive London nightclub.

'It was a bit of fun.' She waved a hand and went on, like an impatient teacher talking to an incredibly stupid pupil. 'My friends and I wanted to make this holiday memorable, but it wasn't to come in your suite—I had to run around the top floor in my knickers. I got caught and ended up in your lift.' Ric did grin this time. 'What?'

'Nothing.' There was no way he'd admit that her impatience was adorable. He closed the distance between them so they were toe to toe and looked down into eyes that had turned the colour of a stormy sky. 'What age are you, Alexa?'

She straightened and seemed to gain an inch, still a head shorter than him. 'Twenty-three.' He could see irritation warring with lust in her expression; perhaps she was still annoyed at his lack of recognition.

But he couldn't concentrate on that now. She wasn't off limits.

Ideal for what he had in mind.

Ric edged closer when he noted her eyes clouding over. The tips of her breasts grazed his chest with every shallow breath. Her lips parted on an almost silent gasp.

'Aren't you a little old for childish stunts like that?'

Stepping back, she glared at him, all trace of desire gone. 'You can never be too old to have fun. Do you even know how any more?'

His tongue froze for a second. How much did she know about his past? There was a time in his late teenage years where he did everything he could to feel alive, almost giving Maria and Antonio a heart attack in the process. But he was sure the worst of his past was buried, they'd made sure their money kept his secrets. She couldn't know.

He dragged his mind back to the present. 'Oh, I know how to have fun.'

Ric's gaze swept down over the swell of her breasts, narrow waist to curvy hips he imagined were silky and firm. Heat punched him square in the groin and he shifted, trying to ease the tightening of his trousers.

'Mind out of the gutter, Castillo, and eyes where I can see them.'

His gaze rose at a leisurely pace back to her frowning face.

'*That* is not the kind of fun I was referring to.'

He cocked a brow. 'Don't tell me you hadn't thought about it. I saw you eyeing me up.' He grinned and her mouth popped open.

'I've just met you!' She looked annoyed, but from the lust darkening her eyes he knew he was right.

Ric chanced a step closer. 'And yet you want me.'

Alexa retreated a few steps and banged into the wall. 'Hold it right there, Castillo.' She held her hand out again, palm forward, an inch away from his shirt.

'Call me Ric.' He reached out and curled his fingers around her arm, her racing pulse made his smile grow wider. 'Your body's reaction can't lie.' His thumb traced light circles on the inside of her wrist.

Alexa's eyes darkened further to a stormy grey. 'It's adrenaline, not lust.' She snatched her hand back.

The breathless reply made his already heated blood sizzle. He lowered his head, hovered his lips above her ear. 'Keep telling yourself that, you might start to believe it.'

Alexa wasn't the kind of woman he'd want a short liaison with—her personal life was too messy and far too public for his liking—but he couldn't deny his attraction to her. Any more than she could deny hers.

She planted a hand on his chest and pushed him back. Ric could see her cheeks tint with arousal and her chest rose and fell with heavy breaths.

'My friends will be wondering where I am. They'll end up phoning security to hunt me down.'

Ric guessed it was time for a cold shower. Alexa headed for the lift. He reached out and clasped her by the arm; his palm tingled at the contact. 'Wait.'

She turned to face him, her eyebrows raised. 'I'm not going to sleep with you, Ric. Forget it.'

If her gaze hadn't dipped to his chest at the same time as she licked her lips, he might have believed her. But that's not what he wanted. This time. 'You owe me a date.'

'Excuse me?' Pulling out of his grasp, she glared at him.

His gaze dipped to her rosy pout, slightly damp from her tongue. Another bolt of heat headed south. 'I have a party to go to tomorrow night.' Actually, he had networking to do and having a beauty like Alexa on his arm might convince some of the old men with too much money and wives long since gone to attend his charity ball in a few weeks. 'And you're coming with me.'

Taking her would be risky, but he'd never let that stop him

before. She was unpredictable and if the media suspected he was having a fling with her, they'd dig deep into his past. Then again, her father's status was well known even here and he could work that to his advantage. He had no doubt she could be charming, he just had to keep her in check.

She laughed. 'I don't think so.'

Ric shrugged. 'Then I'll be happy to call security and have them hold you until the police arrive.' Her brows drew together and Ric continued. 'If you really are press worthy, I'm sure I can arrange for one of the reporters to shoot the story.'

Fear flashed in her eyes, but it was gone in a heartbeat. She smirked at him. 'I'm going back to my room.'

Irritation warred with amusement, but in two steps he was in front of the elevator doors.

She glared at him, then turned back to his apartment. 'Fine, I'll take the stairs.'

'Good luck with that, the door is locked.' He smirked at her and slid his phone from his pocket. 'Last chance.'

Her eyes widened, but she straightened her shoulders. 'You wouldn't.'

He lifted an eyebrow and hit speed dial, then the speaker. The ringing sounded in the room.

'Hola, Señor Castillo,' a voice answered. Alexa paled.

Ric lifted the handset closer to his mouth.

'Fine, I'll go with you.' She glared at him.

He smiled. After telling security they weren't required, he disconnected the call. 'Good choice. It won't be so bad. Fine dining, champagne and I'll even buy you a new dress.'

She crossed her arms and his gaze dropped to her cleavage. 'I have my own party clothes.'

An image of her in her usual style, a barely-there concoction of silk, flooded his mind and his whole body heated up. His gaze snapped to hers and he glared right back. 'It's formal, Alexa.'

Puffing out a breath, she stepped closer. 'I can do formal. Do you know how many corporate affairs my straight-laced father, *Robert Green*, has dragged me to over the years?' She poked a white tipped finger nail into his chest. 'Far too many. And it better not be as boring as those.'

He grabbed the offending finger, used it to haul her body against his, lowered his head and whispered in her ear, 'the night will be as fun as we make it.'

He released her trembling frame, took a step back and hit the button for the elevator. After a lingering glance at her almost-naked body he pulled his t-shirt over his head and handed it to her with a shred of regret. Alexa's mouth fell open as she fixed her attention on his chest. Ric smirked as she accepted the shirt with a shaking hand.

'Put this on.'

Alexa obeyed slowly, as if the sight of his naked skin cast a dreamlike spell over her. Ric couldn't believe it, but in his shirt she looked even sexier than she had in her underwear. Legs that went on forever held his gaze and, even though he knew what was under the white cotton, he wanted to rip it off and find out all over again.

He cleared his throat. 'A limo will pick you up out front at seven. I'll meet you at the event.'

Alexa startled out of her trance. 'But where are we going? How long will it take?'

A ping announced the arrival of the elevator and Ric gestured for Alexa to enter. She did, then held her finger on the open button, her eyebrow raised in question.

He tried not to smile. He'd given her an ultimatum she couldn't refuse, yet she wouldn't admit defeat.

'Do you like surprises?' he asked.

Alexa pressed her lips together as if considering his question. 'Not the kind that lead to a party with the atmosphere of a wake.'

He chuckled again, wondering whether she had a brain-to-mouth filter at all. 'You'll just have to hope it's something better.'

She folded her arms and pouted at him. He smiled as the doors began to slide shut.

'Don't be late, Alexa. And remember, it's formal.'

The clink of metal slamming together halted her not-so-innocent reply.

After the lift had disappeared, Ric headed for the bathroom, intent on taking the cold shower for as long as he could. Alexa fired his blood like no woman had in a long time and she would no doubt look spectacular all glammed up by his side.

But he'd need to make sure he kept a stranglehold on his libido. Falling into bed with Alexa—as tempting as it had been tonight—wouldn't be a smart choice. The girl was wild, unpredictable and far too irresponsible. He knew he was walking a fine line using her status to tempt guests to the ball, but dating her crossed it completely. That would draw the kind of attention he didn't need. Especially if the media dug too deep into his past…

Chapter Two

Wild. Daring. Completely bonkers.

Alexa had been accused of all these things, but it didn't bother her. Ric's accusation that she was childish hit a nerve. She twisted the knob and threw the door open. Jenna yelped into the hotel phone, while Sarah paced the living room. They both turned to her with wild, worried eyes.

Alexa shut the door behind her. The gymnasts in her tummy felt more like heavy weight champs. 'What's wrong?'

'Where have you been, Alexa?' Sarah stomped towards her, a frown marred her brow.

'It's okay, she's back now,' Jenna spoke into the receiver then hung up. She glared at Alexa. 'We've been worried sick.'

Hugging her stomach, she swallowed. 'The dare didn't go as planned. I ended up in Enrique Castillo's penthouse.'

She was rewarded with wide eyes and gaping mouths. Jenna recovered first. 'His t-shirt?'

Alexa nodded, her eyebrows pulled together. 'He blackmailed a date out of me too.' The arrogant, pushy, git. She shook her head in exasperation, who'd have thought he'd actually back up his threat? If it was her father, he wouldn't want bad press for his hotel. Not Castillo. 'Tomorrow night. Some mortuary gig.'

Well, not quite. But it didn't sound promising. *Formal*, in her opinion, meant boring and there was nothing she loathed more than boring. Except having to call her father to ask him to bail her out of a Spanish prison. She shuddered at the thought.

'A date?' Sarah perked up, skipping over the fact Alexa had said blackmailed, and clapped her hands like a loon. The shiny diamond on her ring finger sparkled in the light.

Alexa quelled a grimace as a chill ran through her. Why her friends felt the need to settle down so young was beyond her. Then again, they hadn't been brought up by her father.

'And he's gorgeous,' Jenna added, already on her way to the mini bar. Did neither of her friends hear the word blackmail? Jenna pulled a bottle of Cristal from the fridge. 'This calls for a celebration.'

'I don't think so.' Alexa accepted the champagne flute though— how could she not? The sip she took was heavenly and exactly what she needed right now. They settled down onto the sofas. 'I'm not looking for *the one*.' And even if she was, Alexa knew it wouldn't be Ric. Lush as that chest may be…

'Just imagine. We could all end up getting married this year!' Sarah bounced up and down in her seat, her short blonde bob swished around her shoulders.

The blood drained from Alexa's face and the weight in her stomach felt heavier than lead. 'No.' Her protest was barely a whisper. Bunnies would rule the earth before she married a man even remotely like her father. From her experience, successful men, even aspiring ones, were all the same. God knows her father had tried to set her up with enough of them. He'd even staged a proposal from one. She had pulled on her running shoes and bolted in the opposite direction.

Jenna saved her. 'Sarah, let's not get ahead of ourselves. They've not been on the date yet.'

Alexa flashed her a grateful smile.

17

Sarah just pouted. 'Where's he taking you? You said mortuary?'

Shrugging, she sipped her wine then tucked her legs under her. 'He said formal, which means black-tied, straight-laced, men dribbling on about their success. Might as well be a wake. Those kind of parties are always dull.'

Rolling her eyes, Sarah said, 'You never moan when we go to functions like that.'

'That's different. That's networking for my business. This is a boring date with a boring guy whose sole idea of fun is a frisk between the sheets.'

Hell, in other words. Shivers ran through her again and her body tingled, betraying her thoughts. It seemed her hormones liked the idea of a frisk with Castillo. Well, they'd just have to be disappointed.

'Sounds like fun to me.' Jenna giggled. 'Seriously though, what are you going to wear? You've nothing formal with you.'

Sarah clapped her hands together again. 'We could go shopping tomorrow.'

Alexa smirked. 'No need. I have the perfect dress.'

Jenna frowned at her, unconvinced.

'The bronze silk Gucci.' Her lips curved wider. She couldn't wait to see Ric's face. It would serve him right for blackmailing her into going.

'Alexa, that scrap shows off more than it hides. He said *formal*.'

Suppressing a giggle, she pulled her face into her best innocent expression. 'It's ankle length.'

Still, Jenna was right. It was over-the-top and revealing. But, with her sun tan at its peak, the dress would be a killer, and she'd work on ridding herself of the bikini lines in the morning. Maybe it would teach Ric he couldn't push her into doing what he wanted. Maybe he'd stare at her with that hungry-predator gleam in his dark eyes. Alexa's stomach quivered. Either way, tomorrow promised to be interesting.

Her phone beeped on the counter and she rose, crossed the room and opened her emails. Her eyes almost bugged out of the sockets when she saw the name of the American actress asking if Alexa's business Together could set her up with a companion when she visited London for business next week.

She brought her phone back to the sofa and showed Jenna and Sarah. 'Look at the new client I got!'

Sarah grabbed the phone out of her hands and gawked at the screen. 'Can I be the one you set her up with?'

Jenna and Alexa rolled their eyes.

'She wants a tour guide and a dining companion, not a crazed stalkery fan,' Alexa teased.

'I can't believe she heard about your business in the States,' Jenna said. 'But we agreed, Alexa. No work on this holiday.'

'I can't lose a client, Jenna. It will only take half an hour to set things up. I have the perfect woman in mind.' She didn't mind setting clients up with the opposite sex, she based the service Together provided on common interests, but she didn't think an A-lister would want to be seen with a mystery man. The press in London would be all over that like a rash.

Sarah nodded. 'Alexa, reply before she changes her mind.'

Jenna grumbled something under her breath and guilt broke through Alexa's excitement. But holiday or not, Together was her livelihood and big named clients would mean better publicity. With her reputation still shot to pieces and her refusal to touch her trust fund, she couldn't let a client like this slip through her fingers.

She scrolled through her contacts and found the number she needed. It was great business and a brilliant distraction from the whirlwind of hormones and irritation Ric had brought to the surface. Hitting dial, she ignored Jenna's pout and brought the phone to her ear.

The midday sunshine heated her skin like she was in a just-too-warm jacuzzi, but Alexa didn't care. She had tan lines to get rid of and lying topless was the only way to do it, even if that meant being more wary of low-lying paparazzi.

'I can't believe you made us pick a spot this far away from the bar,' Jenna grumbled as she returned with a tray of cocktails. 'There are plenty of topless women next to the pool; you don't need to hide away here.'

Alexa opened her eyes to squint at Jenna. 'Last thing I need is to be back in the papers, especially with the new client I've just scored.'

Jenna laid the tray of multi-coloured cocktails down on the table between Alexa and Sarah's sun loungers. Jenna then pulled a Spanish magazine from her bag and threw it at Alexa. She caught it, exposing herself to the sun again, so rolled onto her stomach.

'Page three,' Jenna said.

Alexa opened the magazine to the page Jenna had pointed to, and her breath caught. 'You're kidding me.'

The sneaky paparazzi had the cheek to snap a picture of her at Sarah's hen party. Alexa was tipsy and in the process of getting out of a limo, with her knickers in full view. 'Can't they just leave me alone, I wasn't even doing anything shocking. Two seconds later and they wouldn't have seen a thing.'

She wished she could read Spanish to see what the article said, but she wasn't an idiot and could guess. Exaggerated rubbish, since she wasn't as crazy as she had been in her teenage years.

'What is it?' Sarah asked.

Alexa handed the magazine to Sarah, her blood heating with irritation. Jenna lowered onto her lounger with a pink cocktail. Alexa went for the tray, picked up the glass with the red contents, and drained half. The fruity liquid was cool and relaxed her a little.

If she didn't have Together to worry about, she wouldn't care. But being caught with a goofy expression on her face and her knickers on show wasn't exactly sending images of the professional business woman she wanted to be.

'It isn't as bad as the one where you fell out of that club,' Sarah said, flicking through the pages, 'it hasn't made any of the gossip rags in the UK. The Spanish must be short on scandal.'

'Let's just forget about it, okay?' Alexa was sick of being the wild-child. 'We still have to plan Jenna's dare.'

Jenna groaned. 'I'd rather talk about your date with the hunk.'

Sarah dropped the magazine and turned on her side to face Alexa. 'What's his story, anyway? Didn't he used to be reckless, a bit of an adrenaline-junkie?'

'He was as far as I know.' Alexa thought maybe the git would have cut her some slack, since he had hardly been a good little boy growing up.

Jenna pulled out her iPhone and swept her fingers across the screen. A few minutes later, she grinned. 'It's so sexy to see a man jump out of a plane, and all these woman must think so too.'

Alexa ground her teeth. She wasn't going to ask, she wasn't.

Sarah piped in. 'What women?'

Jenna turned the phone around to show Google Image results for a search on Enrique Castillo. She didn't want to look, really. But she couldn't not. In all the tiny pictures, he was with a different woman, rarely pictured with one twice. She tried to tell herself the twisty feeling in her stomach was disgust. After all, it definitely couldn't be jealousy.

She polished off the rest of her cocktail then lay down on the lounger, her hands covering up her sensitive bits from the rays of the sun. The twisting sensation in her tummy turned to an almost low burn, and her already warm skin flared hotter. Puffing out a breath, she tried to wipe the images Jenna showed her from her mind. She really didn't care if Ric had dated, or even slept with all those women. After tonight, she'd never see him again if she could help it.

Ric glanced at his watch again. Seven thirty. She should be here by now. He grabbed another glass from a passing waiter, then made his way through the throng of Spanish socialites to the exit.

The car park was empty. Party already in full swing, all the guests had parked up or their chauffeurs had left. He glanced toward the road leading off the beach. Frustration set in as he saw the empty strip of tarmac before him.

Running his free hand through his hair, he cursed under his breath. Today was a hell of a day for people letting him down. First his events organiser, Lydia, who had a family emergency, and now the unpredictable heiress.

He turned back to the boathouse and took a long gulp of champagne. Boathouse was an understatement. The Castillo holiday home covered at least a quarter of an acre and had its own private stretch of beach. The house itself consisted of four levels, the ground floor specially kitted out as a ballroom to host parties for those who were somebody in the Costa Del Sol—or those, like himself, with a connection to the owners, a fat wallet and deep pockets.

The sound of wheels crunching against the tarmac made him turn. His driver nodded at him from the front seat and Ric exhaled. She was here.

Manuel exited the vehicle, rounded it and then pulled open the rear door. Ric heard every one of his heartbeats pounding in his ears as he visualised what Alexa would look like in a glamorous gown. He'd couldn't help but notice her around his hotel. Scandal was something he wished to avoid if he could help it—even in his adrenaline-junkie days—and scandal seemed to follow her

22

wherever she went. He'd worked hard to gain some respect in this society, and whether he deserved it or not, it wasn't something he wanted to lose.

He'd seen her in non-existent shorts, a tiny cocktail dress which made his blood heat and now he could add *undies* to the list.

But none of it could have prepared him for what he saw now. Taking Manuel's hand, she stepped out of the limo. First he only noticed the plunging neckline and his gaze followed the cut of the material to the curve of her breasts and then further, down to the flash of toned, tanned stomach above her navel.

Fire ripped through his veins. Ric gulped down the last of the champagne. It didn't help.

She turned to him, a smile of triumph curved her hot-red lips, flashing bright, white teeth. He opened his mouth—to say what, he had no idea—but then she stepped out from behind the car door and his mind blanked.

His gaze was drawn down over the clingy fabric which hugged every delectable curve of her body. The bronze silk flowed down to her ankles, but it by no means covered her legs. A slit cut through the material, up past her bare hipbone. The pulse in his groin grew more prominent as he prayed she wore high legged knickers and hadn't gone without.

A long, supple leg poked all the way out of the slit as she strode toward him. He was frozen to the spot and his mind seemed to have crashed south.

Pausing in front of him, Alexa tilted her head to the side and looked up. 'You like?'

Too much.

He remembered his promise to himself. Straightening and dragging in a breath through his teeth, Ric forced himself to concentrate. 'I said formal, Alexa.' He frowned to drive home his point.

'This—' She spun around, exhibiting golden skin he ached to

drag his teeth over, '—is as formal as you'll get from me.'

Her smile, filled with mischief, tipped his libido over the edge. He grabbed her hips and pulled her flush against him. Humour fled her expression as her head tilted back and her eyes sparkled shiny platinum. Ric didn't know what she'd see, but he could guess. His hunger pulsed in his groin in time with his rapid heartbeats. Her pupils dilated, and he knew then he wasn't the only one feeling this crazed pull between them.

'This—' He drew a finger down the silky skin on her naked back, pausing when it met the material over the curve of her buttocks '—is not formal.' Her tremble vibrated through him.

Alexa planted her palms on his chest and her breathing sped. Her tongue poked out and moistened her lips. Irritation forgotten, he lowered his head. As he drew closer he could taste her sweet breath. Every cell inside him screamed to plunder her mouth and take all she had to offer, and he knew from her pliant body and come-to-bed eyes that she would definitely offer, whether she was still angry at him or not. His hands, now settled on hips that were exactly as firm as he'd imagined, itched to slip through the split and find out whether she did wear anything beneath the scrap.

Alexa's eyes closed and her lips parted. His hands were an inch away and his body hummed in anticipation.

'Ric, darling. There you are!'

Ric snapped out of the spell Alexa held over him and turned his attention to his mother, Maria Castillo, who was walking toward them from the boathouse. His whole body ran cold. Alexa tried to pull out of his hold, but he tightened his grip reflexively.

Ric hated being indebted to anyone and the fact he owed Maria and Antonio more than he could ever repay made him uncomfortable. They'd adopted him to protect his past with their name and help him start a new life. He'd thrown it back in their faces, using their money to fund his obsession to find a new high jumping out of planes, speedboat racing and whatever else caught his interest.

Now he wanted to prove he could change, be trusted enough to pay them back by making their hotel and new resort in Marbella flourish. Maybe even go into the new resort as a partner, not just an employee. The fact they had handed him the management of Hotel Castillo after all he'd done made him more determined to prove himself.

'Maria,' he acknowledged. 'I'd like you to meet my date, Alexa Green.'

Maria beamed at Alexa, who he released, grateful for the interruption. Kissing Alexa would have been a colossal mistake. Though there'd been a time when he wouldn't have hesitated to seduce her for gain, he wasn't that person any more. And he wanted that part of his past to stay buried. If what he had done became public knowledge, the Castillos' reputation would be tarnished beyond repair. Dating someone with her bad press would be like digging up everything he was ashamed of and announcing it to the world.

Using her fame to his advantage, however, was a risk he'd take for the charity.

Alexa turned to the older woman and extended her hand. 'Mrs Castillo, you have a lovely home.'

Ric couldn't believe Alexa recognised the other woman. Maria and her husband were well known in Spain for their expanding chain of luxury hotels and charity work, but he hadn't thought the news of their success would spread to London or if it did, that it would be the kind of news to interest Alexa.

'Thank you. Where did you get your dress? It's stunning.'

Ric stiffened. He was reminded yet again how little the silk number covered. It was entirely inappropriate. His irritation returned full force.

Not to mention the way it chiselled away at the resistance he'd spent the day building up towards her. Alexa answered Maria and went on to talk about shoes. He held onto his irritation with a death grip. Inviting her tonight had been a mistake. People would take one look at her on his arm and he could kiss their presence at his function goodbye. After all, what self-respecting businessman would date someone as wild and inappropriate as Alexa?

Flowing champagne, good food and boring conversation seemed to make the stick up Ric's ass more apparent. Alexa kept a polite smile on her face as he stiffly marched her from one mind-numbing introduction to another, his hand never leaving her hip.

Her skin hadn't stopped prickling since she'd seen the way he'd eyed her when she left the limo—the look she'd been both dreading and anticipating all day. The one that said he wouldn't mind tearing the dress from her body with his teeth, then showing her what his idea of fun really was...

Get your head out of the gutter, girl.

Then the almost kiss. Her heart pounded remembering. She'd forgotten that she was still angry at him and submitted to his hunger. She'd even felt the same feral attraction she saw in his eyes, an attraction she needed to get over quick. Thank god Mrs Castillo had interrupted them or she'd have been one frisk away from ending up like her mother.

Her eyes flickered to Ric. He sported a charming smile while he nattered in Spanish to a couple who couldn't speak English. She wondered again why he tensed up when Mrs Castillo had appeared. Maybe he was grateful she'd interrupted them—or irritated—but he looked uncomfortable more than anything.

The fire in her belly, and her desperation to hide it, made the party more interesting than it should have been. Throughout, she managed to keep her business head on and treated the night like she would if she were scouting clients for Together. And she had the feeling Ric was scouting too, but no idea why.

As she glanced around at the décor, she felt like she was in a fairy-tale. Everything was shiny and grand. The lighting high-lighted the white table cloths with pink and baby blue trimmings. A huge, crystal chandelier sporting five tiers centred the massive dance floor and a band dressed in tuxedos played on the stage at the far back of the room. The place oozed money and class and made her a little uncomfortable. It was too similar to the parties she'd been dragged to by her father after her mother died.

'Mr and Mrs Santos, this is Alexa Green.' Ric introduced her to an elderly man with a twenty something year old wife.

Alexa noticed that after he introduced her to Mrs Castillo he stopped referring to her as his date. It was around the same time he started to act like someone had shoved the stick up his ass.

Alexa held her hand out and allowed Mr Santos to brush the back with his lips. His wife threw her a death glare, then turned to Ric with a sultry glint in her eye. Alexa stepped closer to Ric. She may not be dating him, and didn't even particularly like him, but it was rude to eye up other people's partners, and so blatantly. Alexa decided she didn't like the skinny blonde.

Ric's hand tightened on her hip.

'A pleasure to meet you, *novia*,' Mr Santos crooned while his wife remained eerily silent.

'The pleasure's all mine.' She said what was expected with a smile. Her father had taught her well.

'Enrique, the whole place is buzzing about the charity ball you're hosting next month. I'm assuming your presence here tonight is to secure our attendance?'

Trying to keep the surprise from her expression, she turned to look up at Ric. The charming smile he'd worn all night returned and a husky laugh escaped him. Alexa shivered all over.

'You've caught me.' He clapped the old man on the back. 'It's for a good cause. There are too many children living on the streets in

Spain and it isn't the government's priority to help. Your support would be appreciated.'

Alexa ground her teeth to stop her mouth gaping. She wouldn't have pegged Ric as the caring type. Especially about someone he couldn't gain anything from. The fire in her belly morphed into a warm glow. She gulped down her champagne. Damn. She hadn't expected him to have a heart in that magnificent chest.

Heart or not, don't go there.

'Of course we'll be there.' Mr Santos pulled his wife to his side. She looked like she'd rather be anywhere else.

Alexa felt a pang for the old man. He deserved better than a gold digger.

'And I hope to see your beautiful Alexa.'

Only having a week left on her holiday, she opened her mouth to explain she would have to return to London.

'Of course Alexa will be there.' Ric squeezed her hip in what felt like a warning. 'In fact, Alexa's helping me organise the event.' Another squeeze. Harder this time.

Uh, uh, no way.

She wasn't going to allow him to use her, and he had nothing to blackmail her with this time. Her father had used her mother for his gain so many times she'd sworn she would never let anyone do the same. And Ric—the big sneak-freak—was trying to do exactly that.

'I'm sorry, Mr Santos. I'm flying back to London next week. I hope you enjoy it.'

Ric's arm stiffened around her. 'Alexa, may I have a word?' He spoke through gritted teeth.

'Actually, I'd like another drink, if you don't mind?' She fluttered her eyelashes innocently, all the while knowing she was ticking him off, if his clenched jaw was anything to go by. Well, he wasn't the only who was miffed. 'Thank you, sweetie.'

Ric, obviously too straight laced to cause a scene, released her and left to find a waiter—or ditch her. Alexa's lips quirked.

'Trouble in paradise?' The blonde parasite's face twisted into a smile.

'Not at all. In fact, Ric and I aren't dating. I'm merely accompanying him for the evening,' Alexa said, while trying her hardest not to give blondie the finger and tell her exactly what she thought of her gold-digging agenda.

'Such a shame,' Mr Santos said. 'You two make an attractive couple.'

'Yes, Alexa is a very beautiful woman.'

Ric's tight voice sent a jolt of shock down her spine. She turned to him. He handed her a champagne flute, his face impassive. From the stiff lines of his shoulders, the hardness of his jaw, she reckoned his compliment was little more than polite etiquette. Irritation simmered in her veins.

Stick-insect stepped forward then, a sultry smile spread her silicone-filled lips. Alexa wanted to say something rude, something that would wipe the smile away. Especially when Mrs Santos directed that smile at Ric.

She touched the material of Alexa's gown above her hip. 'Where did you buy this dress, Mr Castillo? It's beautiful.'

Mrs Santos ran a hand down the silk covering Alexa's thigh. Her head spun to face Alexa, shock widening her eyes. 'How did you find underwear so seamless?'

Alexa stepped back from the girl's touch. Her irritation had hit its peak when the skinny bimbo assumed Ric had bought the dress. Mrs Santos feeling her up, like she was just another tool to get into Ric's pants, made her blood boil. Now it brimmed over at the attempt to embarrass Alexa in front of the men.

Well, it would take a lot more than her knickerless state to embarrass her—blondie picked a bitch-fest with the wrong girl.

'Actually, I bought the dress in London,' Alexa smirked at the gold-digger. 'Oh, and I'm not wearing any knickers.'

Mr Santos' face turned scarlet, but an amused smile curved his lips. His wife shot another death glare. 'I suppose we shouldn't expect any less from a spoilt heiress, isn't that right darling?' She turned to her husband. His mouth gaped. 'Alexa is the daughter of Robert Green. You remember we stayed at The Crystal? She's in the news all the time for her trashy behaviour.'

The blood drained from Alexa's face as understanding dawned on Mr Santos' expression. If Ric really hadn't known who she was before, he had a good idea now. He remained wooden and silent beside her. The only word she could think to throw back at the witch with a capital B wasn't very polite at all. In fact, she reckoned it would get her thrown out of the party. Maybe even Spain.

Mr Santos turned to Ric. 'I hope your function goes well. I don't think my wife and I will be attending. Enjoy your evening.'

He tugged his wife away as Ric bid him farewell in Spanish.

Alexa had never been so angry or affronted in her life. Her body almost throbbed with both emotions. There was no way she was going to meet any more of the rich and pompous—especially if Ric was going to spout waffle to score guests and try to use her again. It seemed she'd been right about the scouting.

The band began to play a Sinatra number she recognised. Snaring Ric's hand, she dragged him to the dance floor amongst the other guests, all swaying to the beat. Having no other options for privacy, she would have to chew him out here where they'd be close enough to whisper without being overheard.

'Dance with me,' she said through gritted teeth.

'Alexa, if you wanted to press yourself against me, all you had to do was ask.' His tone was light, but his expression was tight and deadly serious. Then again, on closer inspection, the hard lines of his face were rigid with what looked like fury.

'Dream on, Castillo. I want to talk to you and unfortunately, dancing with you seems to be the only time I'll have you alone.'

He slid his arms around her waist and rested them just above her buttocks. Half an inch lower and he'd be cupping her backside. The fire in her roared back to life, but she refused to let it overpower her. Fisting her hands, she rested them on his shoulders, positive if she felt the hard muscle there she'd lose herself and the anger she clung onto.

Ric eyed her balled hands with a frown then pulled her against him. Her breasts pushed against his chest and she grabbed his shoulders for balance. Ric's smirk told her that had been his intention. She stifled an irritated squeal.

His head descended and hovered above her ear, 'Ladies first.'

Alexa's mind muddied when the full blow of his spicy aftershave hit her. With their hips pressed together, they swayed to Frank's husky voice. Still, she fought against her loony hormones and refused to slide her hands along the contours of his shoulders like they craved to.

'Why did you lie like that?'

Ric's nose grazed her earlobe. The brief touch sent the fire in her belly burning over her skin. 'I didn't lie. You will be there and you will help me organise it.'

Alexa pulled back. His eyes were the colour of scorching espresso. His strong jaw serious. The lusty fire inside morphed into indignation. 'Not a chance. I'm going home next week.'

But when she saw his expression harden, his eyes set with determination, Alexa squared her shoulders and readied herself for the fight.

Ric whirled Alexa around the dance floor in time with the tempo. The woman had driven him crazy all evening. The dress she sported covered nothing, yet it covered too much for his liking. He was torn between ripping it off, and wrapping his suit jacket around her. Not to mention he'd been worrying all night that she'd step over the mark, make an inappropriate comment, offend someone or embarrass him further.

And then she'd gone and done it, nuclear bomb style. When Santos, a man with more money and influence than Ric had ever known gave him the time of day, he wanted to do anything to secure his attendance at the fundraiser. Even if it meant spending more time with Alexa-the-pantieless-heiress. Heat simmered in his veins, but he ignored it. Although Santos seemed embarrassed, but mostly amused by Alexa's outburst, it pissed him off. Ric had been right. She didn't have a brain-to-mouth filter at all.

Now, she'd lost him Santos. Ric gritted his teeth. He knew it hadn't been entirely her fault. When Santos' plaything goaded Alexa, Ric froze and waited for the torrent that he expected would come. Instead, she'd kept her mouth shut, even though he could feel the anger pounding off her in waves. Then again, if Alexa had kept her mouth shut about her underwear—or lack thereof—the incident could have been avoided. Making Alexa work for him would be appropriate punishment and would solve his recent problem.

A little into the conversation, he'd made the decision. His party planner announced this morning that her mother was ill and she had to return to Madrid to care for her for a month. That left him up the creek without a clue how to organise a charity ball.

And he bet if anyone could throw a party, it would be the wild party girl Alexa Green. Of course he'd have to supervise, make sure that the party was classy and not trashy, and the close contact could devastate his libido. Still, he didn't see any other options at such short notice.

He needed to focus all his free time running the hotel and overseeing the building work. This party was something he needed to do for himself. He'd lived on the streets, done things he wasn't proud of and had been used. If he could help it, no other child would have to suffer what he had.

Alexa was his only option.

'No, you're staying here for the next four weeks, helping me plan the charity ball. I think that's the least you can do after showing up here like this.' He ran his finger up the gaping slit at the front, traced the outline of her cleavage. She gasped and tiny bumps rose on her golden skin. Arousal zapped down to his groin. Again, he ignored it.

'And you'll behave yourself,' he added, in a no-nonsense tone.

Her stormy eyes cleared to flinty silver. She slid her hands down his chest and pushed, but he didn't let go. 'Don't cause a scene, Alexa.'

She darted a glance around the room, then scowled up at him. They continued to dance while her eyes shot daggers. He grinned, though he was far from amused.

'I have a business to run. I can't drop everything and anyway, why should I? My dress is gorgeous. People have been staring all night.' Her gaze dropped, but not before he caught the shame there.

He gritted his teeth. Men had been gaping all night at the silky skin on display. That was his point exactly. 'Staring in disbelief, I imagine. I'm respected in these circles, Alexa and I've worked hard to gain that respect. Having a woman on my arm so scantily dressed lowers people's opinion as Santos changing his mind proved. You will make it up to me.'

He spun her around. By the time she was back in his arms, her eyes flashed stormy black. 'That wasn't my intention, but I'm not going to apologise for being who I am. You asked me here. What did you expect?'

'I expected more class from Robert Green's daughter.'

'I'm not, nor will I ever be, anything like my father.' Steely resolve hardened her eyes.

Ric wondered why she spoke of her father with such barely contained anger. She'd been born into this life with everything. A family and the best start a person could ask for. Ric had been left on the streets, barely a child of five, with a bleak chance of survival.

The song ended and his frustration grew. He didn't release her. Instead he loomed over her with a hard expression of his own. 'You owe me for this, and you will work with me to organise the fundraiser.'

Her hands fisted in his jacket and she frowned. 'No.'

'Stop acting like a child and take responsibility for your actions.'

Alexa jolted back like he'd struck her. 'I am not acting like a child.' She shook her head. 'I'm twenty-three. Not forty.'

'At your age I started running Hotel Castillo.'

'Explains why you're so dull.' She placed a hand on her hip, causing the cut down the front of her dress to gape wider. His gaze was drawn to the half globes exposed by the material. 'It doesn't explain why you want me working with you. Don't you have a party planner?'

'She's indisposed for a while.'

'The plot thickens.' Her sarcastic tone grated on his temper. She glared at him. 'And my lack of class was the perfect excuse to guilt me into working with you, but you can forget about trying to make me feel bad for losing Santos. I have a business to run back home and no inclination to spend any more time with you.'

'I didn't ask. You will work with me, and maybe even rid yourself of your wild-child reputation by doing so.'

She opened and closed her mouth a few times. Ric could see she was considering what he'd said. He resisted the urge to smirk and pulled her into another dance. Alexa's brows creased, but she didn't pull away. He smelled victory.

Alexa's bravado had buggered off. Again he'd called her childish and again it hit her like a hard slap to the face—harder than when blondie had told her husband Alexa was trash. But she wasn't going to be bullied into working with him, even though she could see what he said made sense. And she did feel a trickle of guilt about losing Santos and wearing the dress.

Not that she cared what everyone thought about her, but if she lost a major benefactor for a good cause, she had to try and make that right. Still, Alexa didn't know what she could do to persuade Santos to attend. Maybe helping out would prove she wasn't the spoilt little rich girl everyone thought she was.

She'd started her business, Together, two years ago, but she knew the money she made barely paid the cost of living in London and she wouldn't touch her trust fund. It was just another reminder that she was her father's possession.

'What kind of coverage will your event have?' She had to ask. If the media didn't hit London with the news she'd helped organise such an event it was pointless.

Ric grinned down as he swayed her to the music. Still, she could see his eyes were tight with anger. Alexa straightened her shoulders.

'It depends how much interest we can raise.' He shrugged. 'I came here tonight with the hope of convincing people like Santos to come. He's well known in society and the more people like him who attend, the more media coverage.' He frowned down at her. 'And while telling men you meet in London clubs that you have no underwear on may score you a date, it won't here Alexa.'

He scowled down at her. She was galled at his arrogant assumption and the suspicion that he knew exactly who she was grew stronger, but now at least she understood why he was angry. Ric was all about respect. Plus, if she was going to do this, she'd need as many people like that to attend the ball to benefit her—which meant hunting down Santos and charming him into changing his mind.

But organising a party this big and glamorous wasn't something she'd done before. Still, she couldn't let fear get in the way. She had planned lots of parties for her friends and herself, this couldn't be much different.

'For the record, I don't make a habit of informing people whether or not I'm wearing knickers.' His lips twitched. 'If I agree to do this, I have a few conditions.'

He cocked an incredulous brow. Alexa smiled. If he thought she was going to bow at his feet he had another think coming.

'For the next week I get to enjoy my holiday. After, I'll have to spend some time on my work. I'll need access to a landline and the internet.'

His expression smoothed out. Alexa thought she saw a hint of relief in his dark eyes. 'All are reasonable requests, but I do need you visit a potential venue with me tomorrow since it looks like the new resort won't be ready in time. A few hours should do it. You can meet me in the lobby at eight.'

She pressed her lips into a firm line. 'Fine. Lobby at eight. But from midday I'm off the clock.'

'Fine.' His dry tone mirrored hers. Holding out his hand, he said 'Let's network.'

Alexa grimaced and he laughed. She knew she had to do this if she wanted the ball to gain international interest. Pulling herself together and remembering everything her father had taught her about how to act at places like this, she placed her hand in his.

Chapter Three

Reluctantly, Ric admitted his opinion of Alexa wasn't one hundred per cent founded. After their agreement, she'd been more than arm candy at the party, and even won over a few couples Ric never thought would attend one of his functions, which almost made up for losing Santos' respect. Usually he kept to himself and avoided social events like he avoided women looking for his ring on their finger. But it was long past time for him to start trying to make a difference to the children who couldn't help themselves, and that meant showing his face in places he didn't fit.

Alexa had been a welcome relief from the constant nagging in his mind that he didn't belong there. Despite her choice in clothing. Heat flared in his stomach, but he vehemently ignored it. She was off limits.

He arrived in the lobby at seven fifty to organise a car to take them to their destination. With the builders stalling while the contract was renegotiated, he doubted the resort would be ready in time. He could only find two venues available at short notice, but he didn't think either would be suitable.

The sound of high heels clicking against the marble floor caught his attention. He took in her attire—which again showed off more than it covered. A black pleated mini-skirt barely concealed the apex of her thighs and a white vest-top cut far too low.

Irritation and lust warred throughout his body, making his good mood take a nose dive. 'That is what you deem appropriate to visit an exclusive venue?' he asked in disbelief.

Alexa smirked. 'It's hot outside. If you have a problem with the way I dress, you'll have to get over it.'

If he took her to Mr Romero's mansion in the hills dressed as she was now, the old man might have a heart attack. Or worse, refuse to rent out his second home to Ric for the ball.

'You're not going dressed like that. Come on.' He turned, sure another glimpse at her outfit would make his suit trousers too tight to be comfortable.

'Wait.' The staccato click of her heels on the marble floor confirmed she followed him. A shred of his irritation fell away and his lips curved involuntary. 'I'll dress how I want.' He stalked past one of the restaurants and headed straight on. 'Ric, where are we going?'

He didn't answer until he'd reached a door marked 'Personnel Only'.

'We're getting you something appropriate to wear.' He unlocked the door, pushed it open then stepped inside. Flicking on the switch, he turned back to her. 'Come on.'

She eyed him like she was wondering if he had a screw loose. With her choice of clothing, he wondered the same about her. He had told her where they were going.

'There's nothing wrong with what I'm wearing.' She propped a hand on her hip and he knew she wasn't going to do this the easy way.

Ric decided arguing would be a lost cause. Instead, he turned and strode over to one of the racks filled with clothes and searched for a uniform in what he guessed was her size. The click of her heels sounded behind him. He grinned again. Handling Alexa was becoming easier.

'Here,' he pulled out a knee length navy pencil skirt, a jacket and a white blouse which looked like they'd fit. 'Try these on.' He turned to her with a no nonsense expression.

Alexa wrinkled her nose as she looked at the garments. 'You want me to wear *navy*?'

She made the word sound like an expletive. Ric couldn't stop his lips from curving this time. 'You're working, Alexa. Not a going to a fashion show.'

She opened her mouth to protest, but he shoved the garments into her hands. 'Put these on.'

Scowling, she said 'There's no way I'm wearing this...this... shapeless granny skirt.' She held the hanger out in front of her. 'Look at it.'

Fighting his amusement, he clung to his irritation at being disobeyed. 'You can't go to Mr Romero's dressed like you are now. Would you rent your favourite property to a renowned party girl in a mini-skirt?'

She frowned at him. 'What's the difference from wearing this—' she indicated the black scrap of material with her free hand. 'To this?' And held up the hotel uniform. 'He'll still know who I am.'

'Appearances are everything. If you look respectable, people will believe you are.'

She eyed the garments in her hands with distaste twisting her lips. 'Fine. I'll wear it to his house, but the minute we get back I'm changing.'

Ric smirked. 'We don't have all day.'

She frowned at him. 'A little privacy?'

Leaning against the rail, he folded his arms. 'Don't be shy. It's not like I haven't seen you in much less before.'

A smile played around her lips. 'Yes, but you haven't seen me without a bra. So if you don't mind...'

Lust arrowed to his groin at the same time his gaze fell to her chest. A number of curses sounded in his head as he realised she was telling the truth. God, was she trying to shatter his control?

Swallowing, he made his way to the exit. 'Change quickly. We leave in five minutes.' He closed the door behind him and prayed for the strength to survive the morning with her, knowing she had nothing on beneath her shirt.

As they wound their way up the mountain in the back of the limo, she gaped through the window at the massive mansion built into the hillside. It reminded her of a smaller Buckingham Palace and the way it spread out over four tiers down the hill made her wonder how long it had taken to build.

With colouring and pillars similar to those of the White House, Alexa guessed Mr Romero had more than his fair share of wealth. This house alone could probably keep all the homeless children in Europe off the streets.

But as impressive as it was, Alexa didn't see it as a place for Ric's ball. Personal parties with friends, family and possibly world leaders, yes. Not a place to raise funds for a charity. It was too showy, impersonal and other than the obvious value, there wasn't anything exciting about the property.

The car pulled up at the front door on the lower level. Ric leaned close and she was hit with his spicy smell. On the drive over his scent had blown out of his open window, but now they were motionless it tickled her senses and aroused her loony hormones to dangerous levels. Despite the air conditioning, her body heated and her skin prickled.

'He doesn't speak English well, so I'll do most of the talking.'

His voice was a deep rumble, all husky and so delicious she had the brief desire to lick him. *Pull yourself together, Green.*

'Try to memorise the dimensions of the ballroom and if we decide to go for it, we can work out the rest later.'

She nodded, afraid to speak in case her voice came out high pitched and desperate. It was bad enough she was stuck working with him for a month, fantasising about the git after he'd black-mailed her twice now was out of the question. Taking a deep breath, Alexa opened the door. Ric's driver stood next to the car, a frown on his brow. She offered him a smile she hoped looked apologetic, but she was glad to get away from Ric before she did something ridiculous, like give in to the urge and lick him.

Ric reached her side and she smoothed a hand over the ugly skirt, trying to get rid of the wrinkles.

'You look fine. Respectable,' he stated.

She wrinkled her nose, but didn't comment. With a hand on the small of her back he guided her over the gravel driveway. The tingling in her skin morphed into a swift burn, flaming over her body from head to toe. Alexa wished she'd worn a bra, that way she could ditch the horrible jacket instead of sweating buckets in the early morning sunshine. After knocking once, he stepped away from her.

A man dressed formally in black trousers, and a white shirt and tie combo opened the door. He looked too young to be the man Ric described as Mr Romero. Must be the butler or something.

The man greeted them in Spanish and invited them in. The entrance lobby showcased a staircase made of glass, moving up and across the hill at every level. She stood for a second, dazed at the sight, never having seen anything like it.

Ric's arm slid around her lower back and she snapped her atten-tion back to him. He smirked down at her, as if to say he knew it was spectacular and that's exactly why he picked the place. Still, something niggled that this wasn't the right venue for Ric's charity. They were led through to what she assumed to be the lounge, if the four large sofas and fireplace was anything to go by, but what drew her attention was the glass wall with the whole of Marbella on the other side.

Mr Romero rose from one of the sofas and Ric introduced Alexa. She smiled politely and allowed Mr Romero to kiss the back of her hand while Ric probably explained in Spanish that she couldn't speak their tongue.

Just like last night, the sound of his voice curling around the foreign words made her tingle all over. Needing a distraction, she sauntered over to the window to let the men talk business and looked down at the city below.

Mr Romero must feel like God waking up on his mountain and looking down on all this every day. He obviously loved the city to have such a spectacular view of it and she could see why. Every building was a tribute to architecture. From the little brick houses scattered all over to the skyscraper hotels, like Ric's parents', it was the perfect mix of modern and old, dotted along a golden beach and light blue ocean.

The harbour was further away, and she ran her gaze over the yachts docked along the side. Then further out to the middle of the water. The biggest yacht of all was anchored in the centre and looked more like a mini cruise ship than an actual boat.

'Alexa, we're going to see the ballroom now.'

She turned to the sound of Ric's voice and followed the men through the house, snatching another peek at the boat over her shoulder. If Ric wanted to make an impression with his party, the boat would probably be better than a hillside mansion.

Ric sipped the glass of champagne Mr Romero had offered, his mind lost in thought. The midday sun shone down from above and the heat on the balcony was stifling. He had removed his suit jacket and rolled up his shirt sleeves, but Alexa kept her jacket firmly in place.

He'd almost offered to take it for her when Mr Romero invited them up for a drink and bite to eat before they left, but remembered the fact she wasn't wearing a bra and the linen blouse he'd made her wear was almost translucent. The fact she must be overheating ate at his conscience, but if he wrapped this up quick they would be in the air conditioned limo in no time.

Mr Romero excused himself to take a call and he noticed Alexa's glass sat mostly untouched on the table next to her as she stared out across the city below them.

'What do you think of this as a venue?' he asked.

Ric had been excited about it when he arrived, but the ballroom in the house was situated back into the mountain and regardless of the size and bright lights, had given him the feeling they were in a coffin a lot deeper than six foot under.

She shrugged. 'I don't see it for your ball. An audience with world leaders, maybe even a few queens, but not to raise money for homeless children.' She turned to him, her expression unapologetic and went on. 'Why ask my opinion? I'm sure you'll go ahead and book it regardless of what I think.'

She was almost right. Her opinion didn't matter as much as any party planning skills he had, but he wasn't sure about the venue and Alexa confirming his doubts made up his mind.

He sighed. 'I agree with you, but I don't see us being able to find anywhere else on short notice. I can't host this at another hotel, especially since I'm in competition with most and I would prefer not to do it at Hotel Castillo.'

Her eyebrows rose. 'Why not? It belongs to your family.'

Ric wasn't willing to admit that he'd refused to live off their name all his life, instead he told her, 'It's the last option.'

Her gaze drifted to the view again. With the sun beaming on her face he could see the moisture shine on her forehead. 'We'll be leaving soon.' He didn't want to think too much about the fact she wasn't wearing a bra, but wanted to reassure her that her

43

discomfort wouldn't last long.

She nodded. After last night's meeting with Santos, he had been wary bringing Alexa to Mr Romero's, but if he was going to contract the property for the ball she could get a good feel for the place. Now, she was a stark contrast from the woman he'd found in her underwear in his penthouse the day before and a part of him wanted her back. Sparring with Alexa made him feel lighter than he had in a long time. She had a young spirit, said what she meant when she thought it and didn't back down from him.

'Who owns that?' She pointed at the ocean.

Ric's gaze landed on the luxury yacht. 'I don't know. One of the residents, maybe.'

She turned to him, a smile spread across her face and her eyes glittered with excitement. 'It shouldn't be hard to find out. Imagine having your ball there. I bet people would be talking about it for a long time.'

Her words painted the picture in his mind before logic could rule it out. He grinned at her, unable to help himself. She bubbled with excitement and her eyes already sparkled with the possibilities. His breath caught and heat jolted south. Ric cleared his throat and frowned at his body's reaction.

'It would be difficult to find out who the owners are and persuade them to rent it to the cause in such short notice.' Business. That's why she was here. It would do him good to remember that.

Alexa's face fell. She turned her head back to look at the boat. 'You sound like a quitter.'

Ric bit back a laugh. 'Not a quitter, just realistic.'

Alexa let out an *hmph*. He smiled at the back of her head. She was every bit the spoiled heiress. Maybe living in the real world for a month would teach her that what Alexa wanted, she couldn't always get.

They arrived back at the hotel earlier than expected, and since Jenna had confiscated her phone just after midnight enforcing the 'no work on holiday' rule, Alexa asked Ric for the use of one of the offices. He'd led her to the room the event organiser had been using and suggested she take a look over the files Lydia had left.

She shifted uncomfortably in the leather seat. The linen blouse had stuck to her torso after a morning sweltering under the suit jacket. She swore today was the last time she'd put on the manky skirt and jacket combo. This afternoon she'd go shopping with the girls and find something less...yuck. Though it irritated her he'd told her how to dress, Ric was right. She needed something more respectable if she wanted to change the world's perception.

It would take a lot more than an ugly pencil skirt to do the job.

The phone on the desk rang and she picked it up. 'Hello?'

'Good, you're still there. Get me a coffee before you leave.'

The line went dead and she blinked at the receiver. How about he get his own bloody coffee!

Returning the phone to the cradle, she stifled a shriek. First blackmail, followed by a severe guilt trip and now this. It was time she had words with the pushy git. She'd agreed to help him organise the ball for the sake of her reputation, not to play skivvy to his demands.

She lifted the navy jacket from behind the chair and slipped it on. There was no way she could walk around wearing nothing but the white blouse. It was almost see-through and the fact she didn't have a bra on was just embarrassing. Being caught in undies was daring, but flashing was mental.

After leaving the small room she made her way to Ric's office and reached for the handle. His voice boomed out from behind his office door. He spoke in sharp, clipped Spanish. The stress was evident in his tone, even if she didn't understand what he was saying. Sadness unfurled in her belly.

Why do you care if he's stressed out? Get in there and tell him you're not his slave.

Alexa knocked on his door, her resolve firmly in place. She pushed it open just as Ric returned his phone to the cradle. He muttered something in Spanish which Alexa thought sounded like a curse word. She'd been right about his stress levels. His suit jacket was strewn over a chair in front of his desk, and the top three buttons were undone on his white shirt, showing a flash of that rock hard chest. He ran his hand through his dark hair, making tufts stand on end. Her mouth watered.

'I'm not your PA. Get your own coffee.' She'd planned on saying more, but couldn't get the words out.

He glared at her with hard eyes, then darted a glance at the clock hanging on the wall. 'Fine.' His accent was thick with agitation. 'I need you here at eight o'clock tomorrow again. We have a meeting to attend.'

His attention went back to the papers scattered over his desk. It was a clear dismissal. Did he think she was going to let it drop? She sauntered over to his desk and propped her bottom against the dark wood at his side. He looked up at her, his expression tight and exasperated.

'I'm on holiday.'

She heard him grind his teeth. 'You also agreed to help me organise a ball. The mansion isn't right, you said so yourself. We have to find somewhere else. I've managed to get an appointment with the owners of *Madame Dior.*'

'Madame who?' She blinked at him, wondering if he'd hired some burlesque club.

'The yacht you suggested. They have agreed to meet us.' A small smile curved his lips.

'How did you manage that?' Yesterday he'd said it was impossible.

'I have my ways.' His gaze fell to the contract on his desk and he cursed. 'And now I have work to do.'

'Aren't you having a lunch break?' The hollow ache in her stomach screamed for food, and she was smaller than him. Surely a man his size had to eat three meals a day.

'I'm too busy for a break and it seems I'll be going without coffee, too.'

She fought the tiniest hint of guilt creeping in, determined to start as she meant to go on.

'All work and no breaks make Ric a dull boy.' She grinned down at him, trying to lighten his mood.

The tension fixing his jaw didn't ease. Damn.

'Is there something else you want?'

Alexa looked at the papers. All were in Spanish, but she assumed they were contracts of some sort judging by the format. He had scored out blocks in red ink and added lots of text next to large paragraphs. No wonder he was stressed. He was a workaholic. What happened to the headline grabbing adrenaline-junkie who jumped out of planes and backpacked through Europe in the summer?

'I want you to take a break. Then you can come back with a full belly and a clear head.' She refused to back down. He was going to go prematurely grey at this rate.

'Unfortunately, we can't all slack off when the feeling takes us.'

Ignoring the jibe, she scooted along his desk so she towered above him in his chair. Going for stern, she frowned. 'You need a break. You're not a machine. I'm not taking no for an answer.'

Surprise flitted across his expression. She folded her arms, staring at him with a look that said it wasn't up for discussion—a look her father used on her like it was going out of fashion.

Ric's mood shifted. His jaw relaxed and something dark and feral heated his gaze. Alexa's skin prickled with awareness and she felt less and less sure about her decision to walk into his office and demand he take a break. She wished she'd just chewed him out and left.

Her heart beat so fast she could feel every one of her pulse points pounding. Her breathing sped when his gaze dipped down to her chest, covered by the navy jacket. He knew she was naked under her blouse and the thought ignited an inferno in her stomach that fired through her body. Suddenly, the temperature felt like it shot up to over one hundred degrees and the cool, creased linen suit felt like an electric blanket wrapped around her skin.

In a move too quick for her lust clogged brain to register, Ric was out of his chair and towering above her. He bent down and Alexa leaned back on her hands. Resting his palms on the desk at either side of her, he had her at his mercy.

Ric's gaze slipped to her white blouse, which was now exposed as the jacket gaped open. She knew he'd see the outline of her nipples. Knew he'd see how hard they were. But that knowledge only made the excitement in her belly grow. Double damn.

'Perhaps I do need a break.' The rasp of his voice sent shivers through her body. 'But it's not lunch I want.'

When he looked at her again, she saw the hunger in his expression. It was raw and scary and sexy as hell.

She moistened her lips and focused her attention on his. So firm, so sure, she wondered if they could be soft or if they would be as hard and demanding as the rest of him. Her body flamed with need.

'Alexa…'

The sound of the phone screeching brought her back to the there and then. Ric stepped back, giving her the air she so desperately needed. She straightened and he looked down at her with a scowl etching the hard lines of his face—like what had just happened was her bloody fault!

She stood and pushed away from the desk, thankful for the interruption. Another glance at the papers covering the mahogany showed exactly how much like her father Ric was, his days of having fun clearly forgotten. Robert Green ruined her mother, quashed her spirits and turned the last few years of her life into a prison sentence. There was no way Alexa would go down the same road.

Ric picked up the phone and muttered a sharp greeting. He pressed a button on the receiver then turned to her. 'Stay out of my business, Alexa. You work with me, nothing more.'

She folded her arms across her chest. 'Oh, don't worry. I won't be in your business at all from now on. And just because I'm helping you out doesn't mean I'm your slave.' She turned on her heel and stomped to the door, grinding her teeth against the dozens of insults waiting to burst free.

'Tomorrow we will have words about this,' he called.

She pulled the door shut behind her. He could say as many words as he liked, Alexa had a few choice ones of her own in mind.

Chapter Four

Ric exhaled in a sigh as he pushed through the swing doors of the hotel a little after midnight. His feet felt heavier than cement blocks. It had been a loathsome day. What started off tiresome had morphed into hell.

He glanced at his watch again. Definitely more than a little. While he stalked across the marble floor toward reception he inwardly cursed his party planner for leaving him and the builders for their lack of co-operation. If Lydia had stayed, he wouldn't be strung tight with the undeniable sexual tension that close proximity to Alexa caused. If the builders did what Maria and Antonio paid them to do, they would have arranged for the water and waste company to inspect the development to check the newly laid pipes before switching the water on—the latter he didn't think was an unreasonable request.

Two days later and he was called over in the middle of the night because part of the development had flooded. The idiots had cracked a pipe when they'd worked on the lower level and now it was flooded under a foot of water. His hands balled into fists as anger clawed its way through his veins, red hot and scorching. It felt like the icing on the cake of a torturous day. There was no way in hell Maria and Antonio would let him buy into the resort now.

He nodded to the night porter who promptly disappeared to

the back room to make him coffee. Frederick knew how foul his mood was since he'd been the one to wake Ric earlier. He pulled out his phone to call his site manager to see how the clean-up was going. As he scrolled down to the number, the front doors opened, followed by a gaggle of giggling and whispers which were loud enough to wake the dead.

His gaze flew to the trio and zeroed in on the shortest, yet most eye catching of them all. In ridiculously high heels and what Ric could only describe as a red mini-dress, Alexa hobbled through the entrance, her hand pressed against the wall for support. Ric's anger boiled over and he rose, left the reception and stalked back across the lobby. His feet didn't feel so heavy now with adrenaline pumping through him.

'My feet are dying,' Alexa complained.

The woman in question bent over so her head was almost in-line with her knees, unknowingly exhibiting a red silk clad rear. Alexa swayed and he picked up pace. He had visions of her tumbling onto the hard floor and knocking herself unconscious— or worse—breaking her neck.

He grabbed her narrow waist and hauled her up. Alexa squeaked then turned her head. Her eyes, too clear for someone intoxicated, grew wide. 'Ric.'

The other two quit giggling and gaped at him, but he didn't release Alexa. 'Glad to see you're not too far gone that you forgot my name, *querida*.'

Her mouth opened and closed a few times before she pulled her scarlet lips into a pout. The lust flared as he remembered how close he'd been to her in his office, how her rosy nipples had shown through the thin linen blouse, how moist and delicious her lips looked…

Releasing her, he took a step back and scowled. 'I think now is the perfect time to have that chat.' He turned to her friends who

51

looked like naughty schoolgirls who'd just been caught doing something taboo. One of them was even trying to hide an open bottle of champagne behind her back. Ric almost smiled. 'I'll make sure Alexa gets to her suite safely.'

With a worried look at Alexa, they both backed away and disappeared around the corner where the main elevator was situated. He turned back to her. She frowned at him, one hand on her hip, the other placed flat out on the wall to support her. Her black nail polish contrasted with the white walls.

'How dare you embarrass me like that!' Those grey eyes muddied, but he was sure he could see irritation bubbling beneath.

Well, she hadn't seen irritated yet. 'We have a meeting early tomorrow. Do you think the owners will want to lease out a yacht to someone who smells like stale alcohol?'

Her eyes burned. 'I'm on *holiday*, Ric, what did you expect?'

Ric's anger boiled his blood. He wanted to tell her to act like an adult, but this was Alexa and he was beginning to learn she did what she pleased. He had to find another way if it killed him.

Alexa met his gaze, a cheeky smirk quirking her lips. 'Are we done?'

His blood hit scorching. 'No, we are far from done.' If he could just figure out how to tame the wild heiress…Ric gritted his teeth.

'If you're getting ready to haul me over the coals, we better sit down. My feet died two minutes ago and I swear I'm going to collapse any second.'

He glowered down at the skyscraper heels. What the hell had she been thinking wearing those for any length of time? The silver spike was at least six inches.

'Fine, my office.' He turned and took a step away.

'Castillo, what part of *my feet are dead* didn't you understand? I can't walk!'

Agitation twisted in his stomach, but he turned back to her and there it was again. The expression that questioned his sanity. He took a deep breath, closed his eyes then counted to ten. When he opened them, he felt calmer, but Alexa had bent over again. Her backcombed bob upturned and her bottom up in the air like a perfectly rounded peach. Swallowing against the lump in his throat, he asked, 'What are you doing?'

'Extracting the Jimmy Choos in the hope of resuscitating my poor feet.'

'For the love of—'

'Gimme a minute.'

He watched as she reached for the strap at the side, fumbling from her upside-down angle. Irritation and impatience warred with the swelling heat in his groin. She still struggled with the strap when his patience expired.

Reaching down, he hauled her up by her shoulders.

'What are you doing?' Ric ignored her glare and pulled her off her feet. 'Put. Me. Down.'

Her breathless reply made him far too aware that every curve of hers was pressed against him. Ric prayed the blood pulsing in his groin would slow before he embarrassed himself. Taking off in the direction of his office, he tried to remember the state of his development drenched by a foot of muddy water and held on to his sour mood as best he could with Alexa wriggling against him.

When he reached the elevator, she looked up at him, her eyes shone with fury. 'You know in Britain this could be construed as sexual harassment in the workplace.'

'It's lucky we're not in Britain, and that I'm not interested in you sexually,' he lied.

His body pulsed to life when she was around. Whether it was anger, exasperation or a draining-the-head-of-blood feeling, he always felt something. And earlier in his office—when he'd lost his mind under the pressure of the negotiations for the new design and build contract—he'd been lost in the temptation of her. Ric thanked god for another interruption, because getting involved with Alexa would lose him the respect he'd worked hard for years to achieve.

'Really?' she asked as she leaned back against the elevator. 'So today when you almost pawed me in your office – that was all in my imagination, was it?' Her arms folded across her chest like she dared him to deny it.

Ric dared. 'I was under pressure and you didn't help by adding to it. What happened in my office will never happen again.' He made sure his face was as serious as he was. 'I don't have time to date any more, and I certainly don't have liaisons with people like you. Forget this afternoon. I have.'

'*People like me?*' Perfectly curved brows rose over wide eyes.

Ric ran a hand through his hair. The elevator doors opened and he ushered Alexa in, giving him a second to think about how to reply. She winced and stumbled on her heels. Grabbing her by the waist, he carried her to the far corner so she could support her weight on the bar.

'Turn around,' he ordered.

She did and held onto the metal bar with both hands. He sunk to his knees and lifted her left foot. 'What are you thinking trying to walk in these ankle breakers?' Shaking his head, he unbuckled the strap and slid it off. He almost rubbed the soles, but remembered his earlier comment. Rubbing her feet would surely give her more ammunition.

'They're gorgeous. Do I need any more reason than that?'

'I'm sure if you asked your chiropodist, he'd have a few.'

Alexa's lips quirked as he removed the other heel. 'Like I said. I'm twenty-three, not forty.'

Ric straightened and handed her both shoes. She accepted them with a smile that swiftly morphed into a scowl. 'People like me?'

'Alexa, you're irresponsible, childish and in the papers every other week. To say you have a less-than-stellar reputation would be an understatement.'

Alexa's grin disappeared. With both hands planted on her hips and the shoes dangling from her fingers, she glared at him. 'I'm not childish.' Unable to help it, his brow rose. 'I'm not. Just because I don't want to settle down, or turn into a boring old fart doesn't mean I'm immature. I know how to act at your stupid functions, I do it for my own business, but in my free time I do what makes me happy.'

The elevator stopped and the doors slid open. He exited then turned back when he didn't hear her follow. 'Do you need me to carry you again?' Ric put his arm against the door to stop them closing.

'I'm going back to my room to soak my feet.'

She didn't meet his gaze this time; instead she looked down at the shoes in her hands. Had he hurt her by calling her childish? Honestly, if he were accused of any of the things he'd said to her, the less-than-stellar reputation would have pissed him off the most. Her public antics didn't seem to faze her at all.

'Later. We need to find a way to work together without tearing each other to shreds. Come on.'

Alexa met his gaze, defiance etched in the firm press of her lips. 'Not a chance.'

Scratch hard work, the woman was impossible.

'Don't make me drag you out, Alexa.'

Her eyes widened and her shoulders squared, but she pushed passed him into the corridor. Following, he watched her try to hold back a wince as her toes curled against the carpet with each step. The progress to his office was slower than it should have been. Regardless of his earlier denial of attraction, Ric couldn't deny his curiosity about how smooth and firm those endless legs

55

were. Like a man on the edge of a cliff, he feared it would only take a slight breeze to push him over.

His blood was at boiling point by the time they reached his office, but his anger had evaporated. Memories of Alexa sprawled over his desk, eyes swirling with confused lust and completely at his mercy made the pulse in his groin more prominent. She paused at the door, but didn't enter. Instead she wobbled down the hall to her room.

Ric let out a relieved sigh and followed her. At least he wouldn't have the distraction of the memory of Alexa on his desk for this conversation. He had to be firm, find a middle ground so they could focus on what was important. Then he could relax knowing the ball was going smoother than everything else. There was no way he'd let his ludicrous attraction to the young beauty overwhelm him.

Every small step Alexa took across the cold floor of the office felt like she was walking on spikes and fire. Not that she'd ever admit that to Ric. The shoes were fab and made her legs look sexy, but they weren't made for dancing. She placed the gorgeous creations on the desk and sunk into the chair he had assigned her earlier, exhaling a breath when her weight shifted onto her bottom.

Ric frowned at the shoes on the mahogany desk. 'That's bad luck.'

Alexa sniggered. 'Didn't peg you for someone who listened to old wives' tales.'

The frown didn't leave his forehead, but his lips twitched like he fought a smile. God forbid he allowed himself to. He may crack that flawless tanned skin.

He sunk into a chair at the opposite side of the desk. Alexa didn't know how he managed it, but the air seemed to suck out of the room and his presence was the only focal point. She tried to breathe evenly. Showing weakness when she had to hold her own against him was hard enough. She couldn't let him see how much he affected her loony hormones.

'We have to win over some respectable members of society, not to mention find an appropriate venue. I expect you to be more reasonable when I ask you to do something and have the maturity to know that you shouldn't be out drinking until this hour when we have a meeting arranged for early the following day.'

The words were so similar to those her father had thrown at her for years. She had to bite her tongue against the petulant retort she'd thrown at Robert every time he'd told her to grow up. Ric didn't have a trust fund to threaten to withdraw if she didn't obey. But he hadn't asked anything completely unreasonable so far. That included his request for coffee, but she wasn't his PA and wouldn't cave to those demands. Better to start as she meant to go on. Getting up ridiculously early was bad enough.

'When you ask me to do something involving the ball, I'll do it, but I'm not your slave.' He opened his mouth, but she cut him off. 'Once my friends go home, there won't be any more late nights. But you have to be reasonable, too. I'm supposed to be on holiday. I promise to be discreet and keep out of the news.'

Before she'd started her company, Together, she had never worried about what the papers printed. If she continued to do as she pleased she'd never get the clientele she needed to give Robert the trust fund back. At the moment it was her last resort back-up. Then maybe it wouldn't feel like she was his possession, like he owned her.

Ric's frown hadn't smoothed out. 'Fine, but if something comes up I expect you to do what needs to be done. Trust me, if Lydia hadn't left me when I have so much going on, I would have found someone else.'

Ouch. First his accusation of her childish behaviour and now this. She squared her shoulders and pulled her expression into

Robert's dead-pan glare. 'Working with you wouldn't be my first choice either.'

One side of his mouth pulled up. Alexa's heart stuttered. She had to remind herself every time he smiled that he was really a blackmailing git. An arrogant man who lived his life for work. A man who she shouldn't even have on her hot-totty radar.

'Yet it seems we're stuck with each other.' The half-smile disappeared and she had the urge to kick herself at the disappointment. 'How about you just...behave how Lydia would for the next month and we call a truce? It will make both our lives easier.'

'Make your life easier, you mean.'

Amusement sparkled in his eyes and she knew she was right. Pressing her lips together, she fought the urge to scream her frustration. Ric wasn't the kind of man to back down. He was a younger, hotter version of her father with just the right amount of arrogance to pull it off. That thought alone should put her libido on ice.

'It will be easier for us both.' He glanced at his watch. 'What were you doing out until this time?'

Alexa grinned. 'Dare number two.'

He eyed the top half of her body with his jaw taut. 'Flaunting your body in public this time?'

The icy question had her chin dropping. He couldn't think she was that bad. 'No. It was Jenna's turn tonight.'

His posture relaxed. Alexa wondered why he would be angry at her for flashing others anyway. He'd made it clear he didn't want her and she had told him she wasn't interested. So what if she did run the length of Marbella in her knickers? Then she remembered. Stick-up-his-ass Ric was all about respect. If he took her to a function to network and half the room had seen her naked they wouldn't take her seriously.

'Do I get to hear what the dare was?'

The smile he threw her way made her silly hormones leap with joy. She had to get out of there. Now. Before she did something daft on this desk. Alexa rose and tried to hide her wince by placing both hands on the table.

'Not a chance,' she told him, forcing a grin onto her face while her feet felt like they would crack under her weight.

Ric rose and scowled down at the hands supporting her. 'Try flats tomorrow.'

She nodded, not willing to argue when her feet hurt this much. It would be a shock if she could even fit them into pumps in the morning. Still, when she glanced at the Jimmy's on the desk, Alexa knew she'd happily take the pain again if it meant wearing something so pretty.

He rounded the desk and offered her his elbow. She took it gladly and tried to shift as much of her weight as possible onto him. Snatching up the shoes in her free hand, she hobbled to the door and down the corridor with Ric supporting her.

He hit the button and the doors opened. After helping her in, he stepped back out. 'I guess you'll have to wear the navy suit tomorrow again. One more day shouldn't kill you.' He grinned.

As the doors began to slide shut, Alexa couldn't hold back. 'Yeah, like that's going to happen.'

His scowl was the last thing she saw. She smirked and leaned back against the cool pole. They'd been shopping and she now had a new conservative wardrobe for her time in Marbella. Alexa had checked his schedule for the month and it was packed with 'mortuary' gigs and non-fun. Still, she was doing this for her business and herself. She could bear the penguin-suited functions and her silly craving for Ric's hot body. Now all she had to do was forget the sight of that chest.

It couldn't be too hard. After all, he had the personality of an accountant.

Chapter Five

'Purple?'

Alexa's skin prickled at the sound of his husky, accented voice. She kept her gaze focused across the road, firmly on the ocean, refusing to turn back to face him until her heart slowed enough to think around the blood pounding in her ears. It was ridiculous the sound of his voice affected her like this.

Ric offered his elbow and she had no choice but to make eye contact. She nearly swallowed her tongue at the amusement tilting his lips. With as little sleep as they had, he looked fabulous whereas she had circles under her eyes to rival a panda.

'Beats navy,' she answered and slid her hand through the crook of his arm.

Like a gentleman, he led her down the marble steps to the waiting limo. All she knew from Ric's curt phone call to her suite at seven this morning was that the owners of the yacht would meet them in a speedboat in the harbour, so she'd sensibly opted for a dark purple knee length dress. It was tight enough not to blow up in the wind and expose her flesh. But standing next to him in flats made her feel like one of the seven dwarfs—Sleepy at the moment.

Ric waited until she scooted over and he slid into the seat beside her. She was hit again by his intoxicating smell, but this time she was prepared. Scooting closer to the opposite side, she rolled down the window and leaned her head against the frame.

He eyed her curiously. 'Do I smell that bad?'

Maybe if she closed her eyes and couldn't see him, the mortification would go away. 'No, my stomach's queasy.' Which was also true, but she could handle that.

His laugh shivered through her and she was glad when the car pulled away from the road. Alexa made herself focus on the reason they were there. 'Tell me more about the owners.'

'Two American men own the yacht. Justin is planning to take Mark on a European tour as a second honeymoon in a month or so, but they have to return to the States for work before that.'

'They're married?' He nodded. 'I'm glad I wore Prada.'

He chuckled again and she made the mistake of not looking away. When he let loose like that his face relaxed and he looked young, carefree and even sexier. She turned back to the window to look out at the tourists setting up on the beach for the day, wishing it was her.

'We have to convince them to trust us to take care of their boat while they're in the States. Justin is very attached to it.'

Alexa nodded and shut her eyes. Yawning, she shifted until her weight rested against the inside of the limo. Functioning on so little sleep was tough, especially without coffee. Even her body's reaction to the infuriating Spanish hunk next to her couldn't keep her alert today.

A hand shook her shoulder a second later and she snapped her eyes open. 'What?' She scowled at Ric.

His warm smile made her heart stutter. 'We're here.'

Stunned, she turned to look out the window and caught sight of two men a few yards down the beach near the harbour. She couldn't believe she'd fallen asleep. Scowl still in place she turned to glare at Ric. 'You could have woken me sooner, now I'm going to be fighting the cobwebs in my brain to concentrate on the conversation.'

He frowned at her. 'If you'd gone to bed at a reasonable hour, this wouldn't have happened. Don't mess this up, Alexa.'

He abruptly left the limo and a jolt of anger chased away the rest of the sleep from her brain. If he hadn't blackmailed her to begin with, she wouldn't be in this position at all.

Alexa left the car and followed Ric across the beach. The two men were blonde, tanned and toned all over. They both had oodles of sex appeal in their swim shorts. The best men were always either gay or married. She sighed. Not that she was looking, but if she was these two wouldn't have been on her no-way-in-hell list. Anyone who'd buy a yacht this huge and sail around Europe for a second honeymoon couldn't be boring.

Ric introduced them and she shook both Justin and Mark's hands. They winked at her and she grinned.

'Wow, this will be the first time we've had a proper celebrity on *Madame Dior*,' Justin said to Mark.

She was about to ask who the celebrity was when Ric jumped in. 'I assure you, Alexa will be on her best behaviour.'

Oh. They'd meant her. She fought the urge to curse Ric out. Two days ago he'd said he hadn't known who she was, now all of a sudden he was defending her against behaviour he had claimed to know nothing about. Git wasn't strong enough an insult.

'We're not worried about that, just excited. The old girl hasn't seen anyone other than our families.' Mark linked his fingers with Justin and smiled.

'Really?' she asked. The boat was huge, more like a cruise ship than a private vessel.

Justin nodded. 'And we're really sorry, but we have a meeting in an hour at the other side of the city.'

She noticed Ric's shoulder's tense. 'That's okay,' Alexa assured them before grumpy Castillo could make an appearance. 'We can come back another time.'

Mark shook his head. 'That's not what we meant. There are two boats here. Ric, you used to race speedboats right?' At Ric's nod, he continued. 'You should be able to get you both there and back. Justin and I will give you a quick tour and leave you to check the place out. If it's what you two are after, you can give us a call later.'

Ric nodded, his gaze flashed to hers and away so quickly she swore she imagined the unease there.

'You raced boats?' she asked. If her mouth hung open a little, she didn't care. Ric, stick-in-his-ass appearances-are-everything *raced speedboats.* She knew he had been involved in extreme sports, but she'd always figured it would be the dullest kind.

Justin chimed in. 'He was one of the best, too. They have a tournament here every summer and four years ago he won.'

Ric shrugged. 'I haven't raced since then.'

She wanted to ask why not, but shut her mouth in time. The answer shouldn't interest her. He was who he was now, and the more curious she got the more dangerous he was to be around. They were organising a party together and at the end of it they'd both go their separate ways.

'I bet on you that year,' Mark added with a grin. 'Won enough to take this dude over to Italy for the weekend.'

Alexa guessed that might have something to do with them renting out their love boat for a ball they had no interest in. Ric smiled at Mark, but his shoulders hadn't relaxed.

'We better get going or we'll be late,' Justin announced and led them down to two speedboats next to the harbour.

After a quick tour of the deck, Mark and Justin left him alone on their yacht with Alexa. She'd been quiet on the ride over. Maybe still trying to wake up, like she'd said. She looked thoughtful, though.

He wished the men hadn't mentioned his speedboat racing stint.

The boat was bigger than it looked from the shore. Justin had boasted an ability to host almost two hundred guests on this level alone. There was a glass room in the centre, sporting a huge bar and toward the back was a stage that would be perfect for the band they'd booked.

Ric had a good feeling about the place. Raising money for the charity was important, there weren't enough Marias and Antonios to save all the children without homes, and having the ball here would attract the rich and curious.

'What do you think?' he asked.

'Honestly, I can't picture you racing a boat. I'd thought that would be too much fun.' The corners of her lips tilted, but her face looked too pale.

'I meant the boat, Alexa.' Curiosity shone from her eyes, but he wasn't going into his crazy adolescent behaviour with her.

She looked around again. 'There's enough room for a decent sized party.' The boat swayed on the waves and she grabbed the railing for support.

'Are you okay?' Her face had taken on a shade of green and sweat beaded on her brow.

'I think I need to visit the bathroom.'

She had motion sickness, either that or the effects of the alcohol she'd drunk the night before were catching up with her. Ric sighed heavily and darted a glance around the deck. There was no bathroom in sight.

'Let's try a level down.'

She sucked in a breath and held it. Ric cursed silently and took hold of her hand. Urging her away from the rail, he pulled her towards the staircase which Justin had said led to the galley. Surely there would be a bathroom close.

Her hand was cold in his and he hoped she could hold on

until they found somewhere. Once down the stairs, he passed the galley and tried random doors along the corridor. One was slightly ajar and led to a double bedroom, but it was the en suite inside that caught his eye. He pointed and she hurried in, slamming the bathroom door behind her.

He hovered at the doorway, not wanting to interrupt the private space or hear Alexa, but the boat rocked again and the door to the room creaked as it swayed. He pushed it shut to avoid the irritating grate of rust.

He heard the taps run, but as she cleaned up his gaze drifted to the double bed covered in black silk sheets. Before he could stop it, an image filled his mind of Alexa in her underwear, spread over the mattress with the same desire he'd seen darkening her eyes to a stormy grey when she was beneath him on his desk.

Closing his eyes, he cursed himself. She was sick, and he had just mentally undressed her.

Working with Alexa was risky enough, taking her to bed would be a minefield. He had to keep her off his mind. She was there to help with the party, nothing else.

The bathroom door opened. 'I feel better now.'

His irritation at his wayward thoughts sharpened his tone. 'If you hadn't gone out last night, you'd be fine today.'

He didn't believe for a second Alexa would choose a boat as the venue if she suffered from motion sickness.

She glowered at him and stomped toward the door. 'I haven't eaten anything today, that's all. I'm fine after that glass of water.'

She turned the handle and pulled, but nothing happened. Ric grabbed the knob and twisted, but there was no purchase, like the knob wasn't connected to the other side. He cursed.

'Why did you shut the door?' She folded her arms across her chest.

A jolt of irritation burned through him at her accusing tone.

'Because it creaked and I didn't know how long you'd be.'

He tried pressing the knob in tighter but it was useless.

'This is the worst holiday ever.'

'Perhaps if you'd foregone the partying, we wouldn't be stuck in this predicament,' Ric snapped, returning her glare with one of his own.

'Don't put this on me. The door was obviously left open for a reason. You're the one who closed it.' She stepped closer, her eyes burning. Arousal flashed alongside his irritation, angering him more. 'And as you saw last night, I wasn't drunk even though I'm on holiday and had every bloody right to be. If it wasn't for you blackmailing me I'd be lying on the beach right now working on my tan.'

Alexa's arms had switched position to her hips in her onslaught, tightening the fabric across the contours of her breasts. Her nipples stood to attention behind the material and all Ric could focus on was the sound of her harsh breathing, the remembered image of all that silky skin beneath and he was a heartbeat away from losing control.

'I didn't blackmail you,' he insisted. 'If you hadn't behaved the way you did, I would never have had to give you the ultimatum.'

She stepped closer, anger pounding off her petite frame in waves. He had a vision of her on the bed beneath him, her wild hair spread around her face using both their anger to push each other to unknown pleasure.

'You arrogant—'

Ric grabbed Alexa around the waist and lifted her up so they were eye to eye. Backing her into the wall, he fought every urge he had to close the gap between their faces and kiss her. She gasped, her eyes wide with surprise as her hands circled his arms for support. But then something shifted in her expression, her eyes darkened and her gaze dropped to his lips.

Ric forced himself to remember why giving in to this attraction was a bad idea. He lowered her to the floor. 'Enough. We need to figure out a way out of here.'

Alexa's gaze dropped from his face, her hands clenched into fists and he regretted the outburst. After all, he had been the one to lose control. Again. Not her. He pulled his wallet from his trousers and slid out a credit card.

'What are you doing?' she asked.

Something he thought he'd never do again, but he had no idea when Justin and Mark would be back. 'Let me try something.'

He slid the card in the gap between the door and frame, just above the handle. After tilting the far side down, he held on with both hands and prayed a platinum Visa card was strong enough to shift the metal release.

'Hold onto the handle and pull when I tell you.'

Alexa obeyed, her eyes wide as she looked up at him. Again she was too close, he caught the scent of flowers, felt her chest heave against him with every breath. He forced himself to focus on the task at hand. Sliding the card down, he hooked it on the curve of the catch and pushed at an angle. The mechanism moved. 'Pull.'

Alexa hauled the door open. He dodged out of the way but heard a crack a second before she cupped her forehead.

'Ow!'

'Alexa, let me see.'

She backed away from him, her hand still plastered to her forehead. Her eyes watered, but she didn't make a sound. The swell of guilt he felt pushed him forward until he pulled her wrist away. An angry red, vertical line travelled the expanse of the skin.

'Come on, there should be ice in the galley.'

He stalked toward the kitchen knowing she'd follow. The sound of feet padding on the wooden floor stopped before they reached the end of the hall. He turned to see her pull her phone out of one of the pockets on the dress.

'My head's fine. I'm going to take some photos and get back to the hotel. I have work of my own to catch up on.'

He followed her up the stairs, cursing himself all the way. There was no reason to snap at Alexa. It wasn't her fault he couldn't keep the burning desire he felt for her at bay. He had to find a way to control himself. He had to help with the clean-up at the site over the weekend, and wouldn't see her until next week. That should be plenty of time to put things into perspective.

After the crazy Friday, Alexa was determined to have as much fun as possible. The weekend passed in a blur of giggles, shopping and quality time on the beach. She hadn't seen or heard from Ric on Monday, and managed to plan out a draft guest list and a floor plan for the boat. On Tuesday she needed to prepare the designs for the invitations to get them out in plenty of time, but she wanted to spend the day with her friends. It was the last day of their official holiday and Sarah still had her dare to do.

Alexa rushed through the sketch and then emailed it to a design company, asking to be sent a few samples. Sarah had kept quiet about her dare, probably because she dreaded it. Alexa chuckled. Jenna had done hers. She'd chatted up five men, got their phone numbers and a kiss from each. And Alexa ran around the hotel in her undies.

She checked her emails at noon before she left. There was one from Ric and she wondered if not reading it would mean he couldn't spoil tonight for her. She was going to make sure they all enjoyed their last night if it killed her. Even if her chest felt tight at the thought of losing her only single girlfriends.

She opened the email and groaned. He had another boring function for them to attend that night. Typing up a quick no-way-in-hell email, she hit send. Ric wasn't in control of her and after Friday she had no reason to go out of her way to help the arrogant git.

By three o'clock, she was perched on a stool at a beach bar. The scorching summer sun shone down from a cloudless sky. Alexa thought it was a vast improvement on the crappy British summers. She picked up the Sex on the Beach cocktail and took a sip.

'Asking for these cocktails is embarrassing,' Jenna grumbled.

Alexa laughed. They'd agreed for the last day, they'd all order cocktails from the raunchier menu.

'I think the names are cute,' Sarah said.

Both Alexa and Jenna eyed her like she was mental. 'You think Bend Over Shirley is cute?' Jenna asked, dead pan serious.

Sarah giggled. 'Yup.'

'I think Bend Over Shirley's going to her head,' Alexa said to Jenna, who nodded her agreement.

'Should make the dare easier,' Jenna said with a wink at Sarah.

Sarah's expression sobered. 'Think I'll try a few more before we get started.' She glanced around the half-empty bar. 'There aren't many here to choose from.'

Alexa followed her gaze around the tables scattered on the sand. She'd heard that this was the number one gay bar in Marbella, which was exactly what they needed for Sarah's dare, but the only men who looked gay were the bar staff. She hoped it would pick up later.

Her phone vibrated on the table. It had taken grovelling to get it back from Jenna, but since Ric insisted on calling the hotel room ungodly early, her friend had caved. Alexa glanced at the screen and promptly hit 'reject'.

'Who was that?' Jenna asked.

'The git,' she informed her friends. She didn't feel like being admonished for not going to the function with him. She'd rather wait until tomorrow.

Sarah grinned at her. 'You do know, hate is the first sign of love.'

Alexa's stomach rolled. 'I don't hate him, I just don't like him.'

This discussion was getting old. Jenna had dropped it knowing Alexa would never change her mind about someone. Ric was hot, she couldn't deny that. What woman wouldn't notice? With a chest like his, Alexa was sure all he'd have to do was crook his finger and women would jump straight into his bed, waiting for further instructions.

Not her. Alexa could see past the sexy exterior into the boring, arrogant, control-freak at the centre. Ric liked to be in charge, he expected to be obeyed and both were traits of her father. She shuddered, despite the warm sun shining from above. Getting involved with him wasn't something she was willing to do. She'd even managed to forget her curiosity about the speedboat racing and the way he broke them out of the room.

'Come on,' Jenna said. 'Let's forget about the sexy hotel owner. There's another sexy guy scoping Alexa out.'

In a gay bar? Alexa turned to see the English rock star's publicist, Daniel something, sitting a few feet away. He winked one sparkling blue eye and grinned, obviously remembering the brief glimpse he'd had of her running down the hall. Alexa fought the urge to groan. He walked over, his golden hair shining in the sun. Sarah nudged her elbow and mouthed *hot*. Alexa agreed, though he didn't have the same appeal as Ric. But maybe a little flirting would take her mind, and hormones, off the infuriating Enrique Castillo.

Shouldering his way through the tightly knit dancers in Beaches, Ric decided he hated the bar. Two hands had already squeezed his backside and he was sure the owners weren't female. He searched the crowd, but couldn't spot the messy brown bob anywhere. Giving up for the moment, he headed towards the bar in the centre, cursing when he felt more sand had found its way into his shoes. Whoever had the bright idea to put a business in the middle of a beach was an imbecile.

As he neared, he caught sight of Alexa. Her back was turned to him, but he knew after Thursday night he'd be able to pick that curved bottom out of a line up. Today, it was barely covered in a hot-pink mini-dress. He picked up pace, but as he neared a man put his hand on that bottom and she turned to laugh at something he'd said.

Ric recognised him immediately. A snake who took innocent woman to his bed then ran so fast he left a trail of dust in his wake.

The prickly feeling began in his scalp and spread down over his body, resting uncomfortably in his gut. It wasn't anger, not yet. When he got closer and saw Daniel Jenkins charm smiles from Alexa, his heart raced.

'Having fun?' he asked dryly.

Alexa spun around on the stool to face him, and wobbled. Daniel wrapped a hand around her waist to support her. The prickly feeling in his stomach heated and spread through his veins. He glared at Daniel, but the other man didn't flinch or release her.

The last time Ric had seen him, he'd just checked out of his suite with the rock star, leaving two broken hearted girls in their room for Ric's staff to deal with. And now he was with Alexa. Ric gritted his teeth.

'Yes, actually.' Alexa grinned at him and held out her cocktail. 'Fancy a drink, Ric? This is a Long, Comfortable Screw.' Her voice was almost a purr.

The fire shot right down to his groin. Ric took the glass from her. 'I think you've had enough.'

Daniel straightened, but he wasn't as tall as Ric. 'Alexa's fine here with me. I'll make sure she gets back to the hotel safely,' the snake smirked.

Ric turned to glare at the man who still hadn't released Alexa. His temper flared, but he tried to compress it. 'Leave us a moment.'

Daniel only tightened his grip on Alexa. She sighed theatrically. 'It's okay,' she told her escort.

Daniel released her and left. Ric waited until he was out of earshot. 'You were supposed to join me tonight, but I can't take you anywhere in this state.'

Alexa opened her mouth in protest, but he pinched her lips together with his thumb and forefinger. 'A 'get stuffed' email isn't a mature way to tell me you won't be attending this evening. I thought we were going to try and get along.'

This close, he could feel the heat pounding out of her body. Smell the spicy, yet floral scent that had driven him mad when they'd first met, again in his office, and Friday on the boat. Feel the damn attraction throbbing in his groin. He released her lips.

'Oops.' She giggled, not looking sorry at all. Ric wondered how many of the cocktails she'd had.

'Alexa—'

'She's doing it.' Alexa's mouth popped open as she looked passed him into the crowd.

He turned, frustration welling up inside him and caught sight of her blonde friend. The woman had her lips attached to a man dressed impeccably in a tight t-shirt and well-fitted jeans. The man was so clearly gay with his purple and blonde hair, but that hadn't stopped the woman. If she was anything like Alexa, the guy never stood a chance.

When he turned back to her, she was grinning at him. 'Never underestimate the power of a sexy woman.' She winked.

Ric remembered the blonde wore a diamond engagement ring. 'Her dare?' he guessed.

Alexa nodded and he shook his head.

'Stop being a stick-in-the-mud.'

'I am not—'

She leaned closer to him and almost toppled off her chair. He grabbed her shoulders just in time.

'Prove it.' Her head tilted back to look at him, challenge and a mischievous spark shone from eyes that had turned onyx.

'I'm not making a fool of myself doing an infantile dare.'

Alexa pouted. The shiny rose coloured gloss made him wonder if her lips would be sticky, or if they'd feel smooth and damp against his.

'How about a bet?'

'What?' Ric dragged his attention back to her eyes. The dark swirls didn't help his focus at all.

'I bet you can't be nice to me for the rest of the week.' A grin tilted the corner of her mouth. 'No calling me childish, no blackmailing me into doing things I don't want to and no more grumpy Castillo.'

Ric didn't think it would be difficult. For the next week he had to work between the development and the hotel. He wouldn't see her much, so she wouldn't be able to irritate him. Plus, if he won, he'd have a few terms of his own.

'What if I lose?' He didn't think it was likely.

'Then this weekend we do something fun and childish.' He frowned down at her and she giggled. 'Relax, I won't make you run the length of the beach naked. I was thinking more along the lines of Water World.'

'You want me to go with you to a water park?'

'If I win, yes.'

Knowing she never stood a chance, he agreed. 'Deal. If I win, you have to act reasonable and mature, come to every function with me and spend all your free time helping make the ball the best it can be.'

Without hesitating, Alexa stuck her hand out to shake on it; a smug smile curved her luscious lips. Ric almost felt sorry for her. 'The bet starts tomorrow.'

She nodded, the grin not leaving her face.

'Justin would like to meet with us for lunch early afternoon to sign a disclaimer for the party. I need you to be ready for midday.'

Alexa frowned. 'You've lost already, Ric.'

He grinned and her eyes widened. 'I've told you to do it tonight, so it doesn't count.'

Alexa folded her arms and pouted. He wondered briefly if kissing her would make her more compliant, but shook off the thought. So much for his attraction for her disappearing. He tried glaring at her for a moment.

'Fine.'

Ric turned to leave, then spun back to face her. 'Maybe switch to water for a while?' He didn't like the idea of leaving her here, half-drunk, with the snake, but she was with her friends. Surely they wouldn't let anything happen to her.

Alexa nodded, her face serious.

He turned his head and saw Daniel glaring at him from the other side of the bar. Ric stepped closer to Alexa, an uneasy feeling vibrating in his stomach. 'He's bad news, Alexa. He sleeps with women and dumps them just as fast, be careful.'

A stormy fire burned in her eyes. 'If you want me to stay out of your business, stay out of mine.'

His jaw clenched. Why did he even give a damn? If she wanted to sleep with the snake, he should let her. The uneasy feeling spread up to his chest but his anger overpowered it.

'Do what you like but don't say I didn't warn you.'

He turned and then strode out of the bar. Alexa wasn't his responsibility and he didn't want her to be. As he slipped into his car his unease at leaving her didn't disappear. Ric pulled out onto the road and headed to the function, cursing himself all the way.

Chapter Six

'Come on, Alexa. Just one drink.'

Daniel snared her hand and led her out of the bar.

'Really, I have to get back to the hotel. I need to say goodbye to the girls and I have somewhere to be tomorrow.'

Jenna and Sarah had left an hour ago to catch some sleep before their flight, but Alexa had taken Ric's advice and switched to water—not because he asked her, but she didn't want to feel like rubbish the next day and she'd had plenty of cocktails anyway.

As the alcohol left her bloodstream, exhaustion crept in, making her limbs feel as heavy as lead. Going for a nightcap at Daniel's room was the last thing she wanted and she had a feeling that wasn't all he wanted.

A voice in her head whispered that maybe Ric had been right, maybe Daniel was bad news. She shook off the thought. He hadn't made a come-on. Still, doubt lingered at the back of her mind.

Once outside, he dragged her toward a taxi, ignoring her refusal. 'Daniel, I just want to go home.' She tried to pull free from his grasp, but he didn't let go.

He turned to her. 'One drink won't kill you.' He raised a hand to touch her face, but she flinched. Scowling, he muttered something under his breath that didn't sound nice at all.

Her heart hammered against her chest, pounding adrenaline

through her veins. The fog of exhaustion began to clear and Alexa wished she had a time machine and could go back an hour so she could leave the bar with her friends. What kind of an idiot was she? She didn't even know him.

'I've had a good night, but I'm tired. I want to get back to my suite.'

He stepped closer and gripped her waist. She pushed at his chest, but he wouldn't budge. His gaze, slightly unfocused, glared down at her and his jaw clenched. Alexa swallowed against the lump in her throat.

'Let me go. Please.'

His grip tightened and her heart pounded. He bent down until all she could smell was beer on his breath. She almost gagged.

'You don't mean that. I know you want me.'

The blood drained from her face. What was it with arrogant jerks who thought she would fall at their feet? 'I want you to get your filthy paws off me. I've no idea where they've been.'

He pushed away from her, but the movement sent her off balance. She twisted at the waist as gravity pulled her down and she hit the pavement with her left knee. A jolt of pain shot up her leg and her palms stung from where they'd slapped the ground in front of her.

She heard him curse. Footsteps shuffled behind her but she couldn't bear it if he touched her. Stomach rolling, she ignored the pain in her knee and crawled away from him.

The sound of a car door slamming made her wish the dim lights from the club weren't the only ones. Hadn't Marbella heard of street lamps? She turned to see a dark figure run toward them. Daniel turned just as the man threw out his arm and his fist connected with Daniel's face. Fear froze her limbs as ice trickled through her veins.

Daniel didn't go down, but he swayed on his feet, his hands

clasping his jaw.

'Get out of here before I call the police.'

Ric's icy command zapped through her fear. Daniel didn't argue or push like he had with her. Instead he walked away into the darkness. She could feel the heat of Ric's fury from her spot on the ground and knew Daniel wouldn't dare mess with Ric in this mood. Her knee throbbed out a protest and she shifted onto her bottom. The chill wasn't half as bad as the pain.

Ric watched until the receding shadow melted into the black night then turned to her, his face expressionless. He extended his hand to her and she flinched back.

He sighed. 'Alexa, I'm not going to hurt you.'

She knew that, she really did, but couldn't ignore the fact he'd just punched a man in front of her. Ric was all about respect and upstanding reputations. Where did the anger and violence come from?

When a few seconds passed, he backed away a few steps. 'Are you okay? Can you stand up?'

She shook off the thoughts and pushed off the pavement. Her knee throbbed in protest and she sucked in a breath through her teeth. He was at her side before she could process it and his arm banded around her waist.

Tears she'd been holding back silently spilled over her eyelids. The smell of his crisp aftershave was the most welcome scent she'd known. The violence he'd exuded minutes ago was forgotten and she felt safe with him by her side, supporting her weight. Without another thought, she turned, threw her arms around his neck and rested her head against his chest.

'Why didn't you come back to the hotel with your friends?'

The anger in his tone didn't put her on the defensive this time. If she wasn't still in shock, she'd be angry at herself. 'He persuaded me to stay for a while.'

He pried her arms from his neck. A stab of pain sent another well of tears spilling over her lids, but it wasn't her knee this time. It felt like a blow to her chest.

'Are you hurt?' he asked through gritted teeth.

A dull throb pounded in her knee and she could feel the hot sticky blood dribbling down her leg. Her palms stung, but more from the slap than anything. 'I've cut my knee.'

'Let's get you back to the hotel.'

Alexa slid into the car in silence. Ric didn't even glance at her all the way back and it made her even more aware of the throb in her knee. It had turned into an ache and part of her wished she was still tipsy, because she knew it would dull the pain. His jaw remained taut as he focused on the road. She tried not to glance at him too much, knowing what a wreck she probably looked. Not to mention the air was thick with his anger, and no doubt every ounce of it was directed at her since he'd already taken out some of his fury on Daniel's face.

He surprised her by taking her around the back of the hotel to a private entrance. Alexa didn't argue, since he had to support her weight with his body.

Ric guided her to the lift and hit the button for the penthouse. Now that she could see him more clearly, the angles of his face were hard, his shoulders stiff and his lips pressed into a firm line. She could practically feel the anger pounding off of him, but he never said a word.

'Aren't you dropping me on my floor?'

He turned to her and his expression shifted slightly, from anger to something else she couldn't decipher. His gaze fell down her body and he winced when it reached her knees. 'Ouch.'

Alexa looked down. The blood had poured down to her foot and stained the gorgeous Louboutins she'd borrowed from Jenna. A big scratch tainted the silver leather. Damn.

'I'll take you back once I've cleaned you up.' Ric frowned, and she wondered whether he was merely luring her into his pent-house to give her hell for not listening to him about Daniel—or for another lecture on maturity.

He was dressed casually now, in a pair of shorts and a t-shirt that reminded her of the one he'd let her borrow, which of course reminded her of his chest. Suddenly, Alexa wasn't so cold any more. Her heart was back to thumping out the mamba but it wasn't from fear. Nope, not one bit. She bit back a groan. When would her body learn?

The ping of the lift announced their arrival and Ric led her through the entrance suite she'd assumed was his living room the first time they had met. The door at the far end led to a long hallway with several rooms off to either side. He opened the second on the right and led her into a swanky kitchen, gleaming with chrome and silver furnishings. The room looked too polished to be well used. Alexa guessed he lived off room service. If her father had been different, she'd probably still be living at The Crystal and would do the same.

Ric pulled a barstool out from the frosted glass breakfast bar and lifted her onto it. After sliding another in front of her, he carefully lifted her injured leg and rested her calf on top.

A bolt of pain sliced through her knee and she bit her lip.

All the anger drained from his expression and those rich, dark eyes softened. 'I'll get the first aid box.'

Startled, she watched him fetch a little blue box from a unit beneath the sink. 'You have a first aid box?'

He grinned, a full blown smile, showing white teeth and making his eyes crinkle. Her heart took off like the blades of a helicopter.

'You can never be too careful.'

After he said the words, his shoulders stiffened and the smile disappeared. Alexa sighed as he rummaged around in the box, pulled out an antiseptic wipe and tore it open with his teeth.

'Out with it.' She folded her arms across her chest and stared him down. Just because she knew she'd been a complete idiot, didn't mean she was going to admit it to him.

Ric shrugged, but the movement was too stiff to be casual and his eyes narrowed. 'I've nothing to say.'

'If they gave out prizes for the world's suckiest liar, you'd win.'

He laughed and shook his head. 'I'm not losing the bet.'

'Oh.' With everything that happened, she'd forgotten about the bet. 'Still, I want to know what you're thinking.'

He wiped the blood from her foot, then slowly cleaned the stains from her calf. Goosebumps broke out on her skin. Reaching for another wipe and discarding the soiled one, Ric shook his head. 'It's after midnight. You said I have to be nice to you starting today, and what I want to say isn't very nice.'

She could imagine what he would have said and she wouldn't be able to disagree. She'd stayed there feeling brave and secure because Daniel had been friendly—maybe a little too friendly if she was honest—but he was a nasty drunk. Or maybe the charm just fell away after a few beers. Of all the silly things she'd done, it was the first time she'd knowingly put herself in potential danger. And for what? She shook her head. Maybe she did need to grow up.

The antiseptic wipe hit the gash in her knee and she squeaked.

'Sorry,' he murmured. 'Close your eyes and think of something else.'

Alexa squeezed her eyes shut and thought about earlier, when Sarah had pulled a gay guy. The kiss had been her own idea 'to make sure he was really into her' she'd said. A giggle escaped her lips which cut off as the sting intensified on her knee.

'You can open your eyes now.'

Alexa did and looked straight down to her injured leg. 'Are you having a laugh?' Who bought navy plasters?

She scowled at him. Ric's lips pressed together but she could see the corners twitch.

'If you wear reasonable skirts, no one will see it.'

'I think that defies the part of the bet where you make me do something I don't want to.' Alexa pouted at him.

He grinned and her traitorous body prickled with awareness, souring her mood further. 'This is your fault.'

Ric's eyes narrowed and his jaw clenched. 'How do you come to that conclusion? I warned you about him.'

Her anger deflated. He was right, he'd warned her and she went ahead and ignored him, thinking he was manipulating her in some way to do what he wanted her to.

He moved closer so they were almost nose to nose, the heat of him and the scent of his spicy aftershave made her blood sizzle. Confused lust swarmed her body and her breathing sped. His chocolate irises shrunk with the dilation of his pupils and Alexa's breath caught.

Trapped between the table and Ric, Alexa felt the ghost of her earlier panic with Daniel.

It wasn't the same.

Despite how it looked, Ric told her he wanted nothing to do with her and logically, she didn't want anything to do with him. But she couldn't control the unease coiling in her stomach.

She shuffled back on the stool, away from him, but it was a shift too far. Just as she felt gravity pull her down, Ric grabbed her by the waist and hauled her back up.

'What the hell, Alexa?'

All trace of arousal vanished and his brow creased in concern.

'Please, let me go back to my room.' Exhaustion was kicking in fast and her mind was muddled between the lust and her earlier scare.

He cupped the side of her face in his hand so tenderly that

81

her eyes welled up again. 'I'll take you back whenever you want, *querida*. I'd like you to tell me what happened just now though. I would never hurt you.'

Her heart bounced into her throat and all she could manage was a shake of her head.

'I see the fear in your eyes. Don't tell me that's nothing.'

She averted her gaze to the granite floor tiles to avoid his searching gaze. For the first time in her life, she didn't have a clue what to say. Maybe it was the stress of the last hour catching up with her.

Ric grabbed her chin and tilted her face back to look at him. 'I'm fine,' she told him, but her voice wobbled.

His frown told her he wasn't buying it. 'I think you and I would end up with a suckiest liar award each.' Her lips curved involuntary. 'Now, why did you flinch away from me?'

Ric watched the blood drain from Alexa's face. He released her chin. If that bastard hadn't hurt her, rage wouldn't have coursed through his veins and Ric wouldn't have hit him. It had been a long time since he had to use violence and he wished she hadn't seen it. His insides were still in knots remembering the fear in her eyes.

'You hit him.' Alexa's gaze dipped to the floor.

He ran his fingers through his hair, rage reverberating through him so viciously that his hands trembled. 'I would never hurt you,' he whispered and her wary gaze met his. 'I saw him push you and I—'

'I don't think he meant to hurt me. I rejected him and he got angry.'

Why was she defending him? Ric sucked in a breath to calm himself. It didn't work. 'I'm sorry. You should have come back with your friends, Alexa. If I hadn't have shown up when I did he could have hurt you or left you alone in the dark. That dress is a hot-pink advertisement for an easy mug.'

He'd seen what kind of monsters lurked in the shadows, albeit in Madrid. He had the scars to prove it. There'd been a time when he'd have done anything to escape it, and he had. He'd sold his body and his soul for a place to stay and food in his stomach. The memories shivered through his blood and guilt and self-disgust joined his fury.

He knew he shouldn't have left her at the bar. Knew it the second her friends had stumbled into the hotel without her. Instead of going straight to his office, he'd accessed his PC from the reception and worked there, feeling a shred of responsibility for her well-being all the while knowing she wasn't his to look after—nor did he want her to be. But he couldn't have left her alone drunk, like her friends had done, with the snake.

'I should have listened to you earlier,' she whispered.

It was so out of character, he was sure he'd misheard. 'What did you say?'

She looked at him then, her eyes sad and distant. 'I said *I should have listened to you*. Are you happy?'

The defeat in her voice dissolved his anger. Dark circles were visible under heavy lidded eyes and Ric knew it was time to call it a night. 'No, I'm not happy,' he told her, his voice softer now. 'But I'm glad you're back safe.'

Unable to resist, he tucked her hair behind her ears and held her face between his palms. 'Alexa, you have to be careful at night. Spain has just as many thugs as London, maybe more.'

She swallowed and nodded. Her eyes morphed back to stormy grey and Ric felt the pull to close the distance between them deep in his gut. He released her and stepped back. The draw that pulsed between them now had nothing to do with lust and in his mind that was more dangerous than the desire to have her naked in his bed. Assuring himself it was only the emotions of seeing her on her hands and knees on the ground, the terror in her pale face and the fact she could have been hurt worse if he hadn't got there in time, he held out his hand.

'Come on, I'll take you back to your apartment.'

Indecision seemed to flicker across her face, but after a second she took his outstretched hand and slid off the bar stool onto her right leg. He waited until she tried to take a step. Wincing, Alexa leaned her weight back onto her good limb.

Ric's heart gave a painful beat in his chest. Without thinking about it, he picked her up, an arm under her knees and another supporting her shoulders.

'What are you doing?'

He strode through his home toward the elevator. 'Taking you back to your room. Do you have ice?'

Alexa pouted. 'I can walk, you know.'

'Didn't look like it to me. Ice?'

She nodded. He paused by the elevator and Alexa hit the button. With her warm body pressed against him and that dress hiking too far up her thighs, Ric hoped his zinging blood didn't rush south. To distract himself, he watched the numbers above the doors climb up.

'I wanted to see my friends to the airport today.'

Ric glanced down to see her attention was on the elevator doors. He knew they were leaving in a few hours and with the last minute change of venue, he and Alexa would have to work twice as hard to get everything organised in time.

'We can't put off Mark and Justin.'

She didn't look at him, merely nodded and twiddled her thumbs. A twinge of guilt swelled in his stomach as he stepped into the elevator. It reached his chest by the time he'd settled her on the sofa in her suite with a bag of ice.

'I'll tell them you had important work to do. I'll see you when

I get back.'

Alexa's lips parted and her eyebrows shot up.

'See, I can be nice.' He grinned at her before he left.

When Ric arrived back in his suite, he stripped off and fell straight into his bed without bothering to shower. The guilt had lifted, but as he gazed at the ceiling and willed sleep to come, the pull he'd felt toward her earlier still tugged at him. Whatever way he looked at it, a fling with Alexa wouldn't work. She'd drive him up the wall and he'd lose all the respect he'd tried so hard to deserve over the years—like he would have done tonight if anyone had seen him plant a fist in that creep's face. Not to mention the fact that it might cause enough of a media stir to trawl through his past. No, a fling with her was a risk he wasn't willing to take.

Chapter Seven

Ric's office door flew open.

He rose from the desk when the handle knocked a lump of plaster from the wall. Angry fire clawed through him. Alexa hobbled into his office in a pair of tight shorts, dragging two purple suitcases with a pink duffle slung over her shoulder.

His gaze dropped to her bruised knee and he felt a shred of the anger dissipate, but not enough when he saw the crumbled plaster dusting his floor.

'You better have a good reason for destroying my wall.'

His voice held enough animosity to put fear into the most unruly employee. When he looked up at her face, he saw her eyes blaze like icy grey shards.

'I have a good reason, alright.' Alexa pulled the duffle bag off and dumped it on the floor. She hobbled over to his desk, one hand on her hip. 'Where exactly do you expect me to sleep for the next three weeks?'

Her question, as well as the three bags of her possessions confused him. 'In your room, of course.'

'Really?' She'd managed to reach his desk now and planted both palms on the mahogany. It looked like she was back to her normal self, the vulnerability he'd glimpsed last night gone. Bending closer, she said, 'You might want to tell your snotty receptionist that.'

Ric's stomach balled into a knot. 'What did Sonia tell you?'

Alexa's nose wrinkled. '*Sonia* told me to get out. That the suite was booked up for a month as of today. Didn't you tell them I was staying on?'

She threw him the look that questioned his idiocy. Anger pitched like a fork in his gut. He lifted up the phone on the desk and hit the number for reception. Sonia answered and he asked her in Spanish what was going on. After she explained they had over-booked, Ric checked on his computer and confirmed it. There was nothing available for at least a month. Nowhere for Alexa to stay.

He wanted to yell at Sonia to fix it, to find Alexa somewhere even if it was in the basement, but the evidence was on his screen in black and white and he knew Alexa would never live in a basement. With a sigh, he told Sonia to find out who had double booked. He'd deal with the staff later. Now he had an angry heiress who didn't listen to reason to calm down.

'Well?'

Ric raked a hand through his hair. 'Someone overbooked for the next few weeks.'

Alexa nodded, then bent down to the pink bag and unzipped it. She pulled out a purse. 'Okay. Give me a call when you've found somewhere for me to stay. You can take my bags.'

'I don't think so. We need to nail down the guest list, fix the floor plan and a million other things.'

She stomped back to his desk, one hand on her hip. 'I've spent the morning packing all my stuff with a housekeeper rushing me. I'm starving and I'm going to grab lunch. This is your hotel's mistake so you can deal with it.'

His temper sizzled but Ric knew she was right. If it wasn't for someone's clerical error, Alexa wouldn't have to move. It still didn't mean he was happy about her leaving, nor about knocking a chunk out of the wall. Remembering the bet, he decided caving to her demands was preferable to spending this weekend in Hell disguised as fun.

'Fine. I'll call you soon.'

With a smirk, Alexa left and Ric turned to his computer. He searched estate agents and hotels in Marbella. Three hours later and more phone calls than he could count and his mood was sourer than ten day old milk. All hotels in the city were fully booked due to it being peak season, as were the apartments and villas. Raking a shaky hand through his hair, he realised she was going to have to stay with him until he could rework some of the bookings here or at his other hotel across the city. He prayed there was at least one cancellation within the next week.

After arranging for her luggage to be moved, he pulled out his phone and dialled her number.

'Have you found me somewhere to stay?'

Not even a greeting. 'Yes. Now will you come back to work?'

She paused for a beat. 'My stuff?'

Ric gritted his teeth. He knew she wouldn't be happy to stay with him. Better to save it until later, when she'd calmed down. 'In your room. Come straight to the office. I need to go over a few things with you before I go over to the site.'

He knew it was the cowardly way out, but he'd rather wait until tonight for a blow-out. Besides, she wouldn't be staying with him for long. At least he hoped she wouldn't.

'I'll be there soon.'

Sliding the phone onto the cradle, he wondered if there was any way he could feign a business trip until a room became available for her. But he had too much to do. The building work needed his focus, and he had enough functions coming up to keep him firmly in Marbella.

Later, when he returned to the hotel, the rest of the day passed by in a whir of phone calls and meetings. When a knock sounded at his door, his gaze lifted to the time on his PC. It was after six and he hadn't stopped for a break. His stomach growled as he shouted 'Come in.'

Ric was surprised to see Alexa enter. Usually she didn't wait for permission. She still wore the shorts and vest combo. He kept his gaze on her face. The dark smudges beneath her heavy lidded eyes made him wonder if she'd slept at all last night. His chest felt tight as he remembered her on the ground, remembered her fear.

'I have a few things to run by you before I settle into my room.' Alexa strolled towards his desk and sat down.

He thought now was as good a time as any to drop the bomb about her room, but she distracted him by placing a file on his desk. He looked down to see a list of names—some he recognised as high rollers in Spanish society, others took him longer to figure out.

'What makes you think Londoners would help the children here?' he asked, wondering if she was completely stupid. He doubted any of the additions Alexa had made to the guest list would care.

'They are coming. I've already asked them.'

Ric blinked at her, unable to decipher how she'd done it.

She grinned. 'I'm not without resources. I thought if I could get the big dogs in the UK to take interest in your charity, the media coverage would spread.'

And her reputation as an aide in organising the event would help overshadow the bad press. 'How did you convince them to come?'

'I asked them.' She shrugged. 'I bump hips with them all at parties and some are my clients.'

'What kind of business do you run?' he asked, picking up the list again. He still couldn't believe it. He reached for the folder she'd dropped.

'Together does what it says on the tin. I—'

'I didn't approve these.'

Ric pulled out the invitations she'd had printed at some point. He could tell it hadn't been Lydia: not only would she have asked permission before drafting something up, she would never have used the phrase 'glitziest charity ball ever.' His irritation spiked and he glared at her.

She squared her shoulders. 'I only had a handful made. Enough to send out to the English guests. The ball's only a few weeks away. We need to get invitations out pronto.'

He frowned at her. 'I get final approval on anything you send out. This…' he waved the card in front of her face 'Isn't what I had in mind.'

'You asked me to help and I did.' She pushed up from the desk. 'I like the invitations and they're practically what Lydia had, only more—'

'Do not say fun.'

'Well, they are.' She scowled at him. 'What is your problem with fun? Weren't you allowed to have any when you were a child?'

'No, Alexa. I was too busy trying to find somewhere safe to sleep at night.'

Her mouth dropped open on a gasp and Ric's stomach crashed to his feet. He hadn't meant to say that out loud, but she irritated him to the point where he lost control over what came out of his mouth. Her lack of brain-to-mouth filter must be contagious.

'Ric, I'm so sorry.'

Rising, he shuffled the new version of the contract together and stuffed it in his briefcase. 'Forget about it. I have.'

Her hand circled his wrist and his gaze jerked up to hers. Moisture sparkled in her eyes, but he didn't see pity. She was frowning and her lips twisted as if in displeasure. 'Is that why you started the charity, because you grew up on the streets?'

Convincing himself he'd imagined the horror in her voice, he pulled out of her grip. 'I'm sure I told you before to stay out of my business.'

Alexa looked at him like he'd slapped her and guilt pooled like acid in a stomach twisted by old memories. He pulled a key from his suit jacket and handed it to her. 'This will get you into your room.'

Ric strode to the door without a backward glance. She stirred up his perfectly cool life, resurrected memories best kept forgotten and made him *feel*. Anything. Everything. He gritted his teeth as he realised he would have to spend time with her day and night unless he took up a hobby. For now, something to eat and a few hours more at the office should be enough time for her to calm down, get used to the idea of staying in his suite and hopefully fall asleep.

'What's my room number?' she asked.

He turned around at the doorway, his chest and shoulders tight. 'The penthouse.' She opened her mouth to speak, all moisture gone from her stormy eyes. 'We'll talk about it later, Alexa. It's all there is for now.'

She studied his face, the storm seemed to calm in her eyes and then she nodded.

He left the room and made his way to the kitchen for a quick meal before he got back to work. Still, his hunger had vanished.

Alexa always argued with him. She never backed down. The slip of the tongue about his past had changed that. Ric had to put things back on even ground. He didn't want her pity, or her horror at what he'd survived. There were enough of those demons from his past still haunting him. When he got back to the penthouse, he'd lay down new ground rules.

Alexa stared at the huge plasma TV without really seeing the images on the screen. She'd lost track of the amount of time she'd sat there—probably still in shock from finding out a little about his past. The cream leather suite cooled with the dropping temperature and she felt it seep into her skin, raising goosebumps. Shivering, she rose and went through to the room where Ric had left her luggage.

There was nothing she could fault in the room. The luxurious bedspread felt silky to the touch, the mattress dipped under her weight just enough so that she wanted to curl up and purr. Better yet, the en suite meant she didn't have to share a bathroom with Ric.

She slipped into a pair of leggings and a long pullover wondering what his life had been like before the Castillos had adopted him. He must have faced some horrors growing up on the streets.

As she washed her face and brushed her teeth, she remembered him warning her that Spain had as many thugs as London. Did he meet them? She shuddered. At least now she could guess where his violence came from and where he learned the credit card in the door trick.

Glancing around the plush room, Alexa tried to call on some anger, some fury at having to stay in his home. It was his hotel's fault, and them spending time together was tense at the best of times. The fact that he must really not have any other options dissolved some of the irritation, but his accidental confession pushed it down till she was left cold.

The clanking of the lift sparked jitters in her belly. She thought about going through to the lounge, making herself at home on the cold sofa but she stopped herself. If she saw him, she'd want to know. Everything. And Ric's cool brush off in his office told her it wasn't a topic for conversation.

'Alexa,' he called from the lounge.

She eyed the bed, wondering if she dove under the sheets she'd be able to keep her hammering heart at bay enough to feign sleep.

Footsteps sounded in the hall and she crossed to the door, pulled it wide and planted a hand on her hip. She thought if she acted like things were normal, she could forget about his past and start seeing him as someone no different from her father. But Robert Green hadn't had to deal with homelessness. Like her, he'd been born into the world with more money than he needed.

Ric still wore his dark suit, the white shirt rumpled and his tie had vanished. His hair framed his face in wild tufts and the shadows under his eyes made her heart melt. It took all her willpower to scowl at him instead of running him a hot bath and offering to make him something to eat.

His jaw clenched and he stopped a few feet away. 'We need to talk.'

'You want to talk now, after spending the day letting me think that you had a room for me to stay in?'

Anger was good. It made her forget about taking care of him—not that Ric needed her care. Alexa guessed anyone who survived what he had could look after themselves.

'Kitchen.' He walked passed her.

She heard the fridge clink open and then a thud as a bottle hit the counter and scurried in after him. Ric poured a huge shot of malt and downed it in one gulp. As he reached for the bottle again, Alexa interrupted him.

'That bad a day?' He turned to her, his expression unreadable. Alexa swallowed. 'Drink won't make me disappear.' She tried to lighten his mood with humour but that didn't seem to work either.

Ric poured another glass, then turned to lean against the worktop. 'Take a seat,' he instructed before bringing the tumbler to his lips and taking a sip this time. 'If you're going to be under my roof for the next three weeks, we need to set ground rules.'

Slumping onto the chair, she ground her teeth against the bollocking she wanted to throw at him. Under his roof. Biting her tongue, she consoled herself that now she didn't feel sorry for the little boy who grew up on the streets or wonder what happened to him. No, now she saw the kind of man her father was. An arrogant, bossy, blackmailing, control-freak. Hot chest or not, Alexa was pleased to feel nothing other than anger. Looked like her hormones had finally acquired some common sense.

'There will be no partying. If you're not back by ten, the elevator will be locked and you won't be able to come in.'

'A ten o'clock curfew! Are you serious?' Unbelievable. He was worse than Robert.

'Yes. And under no circumstances will you bring anyone back.'

Alexa thought her body would explode with the anger burning through her veins. She couldn't believe he assumed she would bring men back here and have sex with them, and the inflection in his tone said that's exactly what he meant.

Well, he could think again. She got up and stormed across the cold tiles. Poking a finger into his chest, she said, 'Honestly Ric, if I want to sleep with some hottie I meet at a bar, I wouldn't bring him back here for you to ruin the mood.'

His eyes darkened in a way that had her brain screaming at her to shut up, that pushing him would be dangerous, but the words slipped out anyway. 'And as for the curfew, I'm not sixteen. How do you expect me to meet all these men you think I'll bring back to your home if I have to be in ridiculously early?'

His chocolate eyes, usually warm, now looked like they'd scorch the sockets. With a rigid jaw, he bent down so his lips were an inch from hers. Alexa's hormones exploded like fireworks, but the anger hadn't gone. No, the lust just ignited it further. She wanted to strangle him, wanted to kiss him and bite his lips, wanted… something.

'You're walking down a dangerous path, *querida*.' The husky tone held a note of warning.

But Alexa had never listened to warnings and even if she wanted to stop, she couldn't. If she didn't get out what she needed to, she felt like she'd stop breathing with the pressure inside.

'And you don't have the right to control me, it's my life. I'll live it as I please. I am doing you a favour. If I wanted to go out and sleep with all the men in Spain—'

Ric hauled her against his chest and his lips crushed down on hers. The pressure inside her erupted into molten heat, bubbling through her veins. She fisted her hands in his hair and kissed him back, meeting his hunger with her own. When his tongue forced its way into her mouth, she sucked it in further. Her knees weakened at the taste of him.

Pushing away from the counter, he spun their bodies and then shoved her against the fridge, never letting up on the assault on her mouth. She didn't care, not now. Not when his taste made her burn all over and the place between her thighs throb with increasing need.

His hands slid under her top, right up to her naked breasts. He skimmed the curve beneath with each thumb. Knees weak, she sagged against the fridge, her head thumping off the chrome as she panted. He hadn't even really touched her yet and she was on the edge, ready to explode.

Those lips eased up on hers. He trailed softer kisses along her jaw, down the column of her throat to the base, at the same time he teased her hardened nipples. A whimper escaped her lips. If the blood wasn't pounding in every one of her pulse points, she'd probably have blushed at the sound she made.

Both their haggard breathing filled the room as his hands and lips focused on her intently. Alexa's mind fogged—or maybe she'd lost common sense—because the only thing she could think about was the fact that they both wore too many clothes.

Ric lifted his head and she glimpsed his feral hunger but, before she could consider it, he whipped her top right over her head.

95

His gaze fell to her breasts which swelled in an attempt to get closer to him.

'*Eres muy hermosa.*'

She wanted to ask what he said, wanted his lips back on her. Ric reached for her and she'd have met him half-way if she thought her legs would work. His shaking hand froze and his gaze lifted from her chest. She could see indecision, pain, tightening his expression.

Well, maybe the bastard should have thought about it before he stuck his tongue down her throat.

The molten heat morphed into cold sludge in her veins. She covered her breasts with an arm, ignoring the painful jolt in her heart. Bending down, she picked up her jumper and tugged it on. Ric walked back to the counter and downed another glass of liquor. Her eyes pricked and for the first time in her life, she felt truly rejected. Oh, she'd known her father hadn't loved her, not really, but he still needed her to do his bidding. Ric didn't want to want her, which hit her stomach like a heap of bricks. Even though she didn't want to want him either.

'I suppose that was my fault too?' she asked, folding her arms across her breasts in the hope of hiding her arousal. *Bloody hormones.*

'No.' His voice sounded rough. With his back to her, he went on, 'That can't happen again. You and I…' Ric shook his head.

Alexa rubbed her chest in the hope it would take away the pain. She was too young to have a heart attack. 'Would be a mistake,' she finished for him. The words sounded right and it was what she really wanted. It didn't stop the hurt though.

A part of her mind wondered if Sarah had been right, if her feelings for Ric would grow into something more. No.

He turned to her, his gaze searched her face. Twice he'd seen her almost naked and he'd still managed to reject her. Nothing like that to give a girl a complex.

'Yes, it would.'

He looked relieved by her agreement. Maybe the turmoil inside didn't show on her face. 'You lost the bet.' Just like she knew he would.

Ric nodded, a sober expression on his face. She turned and went back to her room. Sinking into the silky sheets, the bed didn't make her want to purr this time. Everything was going to hell and nothing made sense any more.

He wasn't who she thought he was, or at least not completely. What man could walk away from a willing woman when he'd been so aroused? And he had been, she'd felt it hard against her stomach. She pressed her face into the pillow to muffle her scream.

Even the thought of dragging him to Water World didn't cheer her up. He'd surely hate it but what was the point in goading him? She couldn't sum up the will to torture him even though he was torturing her. And now she knew he'd prefer to go without rather than sleep with her.

Rolling over again to find a comfier spot on the bed, Alexa wondered what it was about her that repelled him so completely. She didn't have a petite frame but, from that first day he'd caught her here in his penthouse, she knew her body wasn't the problem. That only meant that it had to be her reputation and personality.

Squeezing her eyes shut she tried to summon her earlier anger but she felt like a balloon that had just been popped. Alexa knew these three weeks would probably be the longest of her life.

Chapter Eight

By Friday morning, Alexa hadn't seen Ric once since the kiss. She didn't know whether to feel disappointed or elated but her heart swayed toward the former. Running two hands down the front of her pencil skirt, she smiled, knowing that this was a skirt he'd approve of. It was long enough to hide the navy plaster on her knee.

She pushed the door to the bistro open and gave the server her name. He escorted her past linen covered tables through to the terrace at the other side. The summer sun had cooled off a bit today, so the suit jacket wasn't too much to lunch in and she wanted to look as respectful as possible for this meeting. Charm, innocence and making a better second impression.

Mr Santos rose from the table and pulled out the chair opposite. With a warm smile, Alexa slid into it and did her best to ignore the butterflies swarming in her stomach.

'It seems you are just as beautiful in a suit as you are a dress, Miss Green.'

Her stomach dipped remembering the dress and the way she'd acted at the first function Ric had taken her to. Hoping she could change his mind by showing a different side of herself, she said, 'Thank you, Mr Santos.'

He nodded and then filled her glass with wine. 'I am surprised to have received the request to meet after our last encounter, but I can't deny my curiosity.'

Bringing the wine to her lips, she sipped the fruity liquid wishing she could down the whole lot. Maybe then her hands would stop shaking.

'I wanted to personally apologise for my behaviour at the party.' And now that she had an idea of how much it meant to Ric, she wanted Santos to reconsider and come to the charity ball.

Mr Santos nodded. 'I accept, but is that the only reason you asked to meet?'

He gazed at her over the rim of the glass and she knew he was assessing her body language. Fighting the urge to swallow she smiled.

'Not the only reason. I'd like you and your wife to reconsider Mr Castillo's invitation.' She had a freshly printed one in her bag, sans the 'fun' part.

'Miss Green, my wife thinks associating ourselves with you will taint her reputation.'

Alexa's heart thumped out an unsteady beat. She wished the stick insect was there so she could pitch the remainder of her wine over her peroxide mane. Instead, she smiled warmly.

'I understand. The British media love a good story and I've never given them a reason not to follow me.' For the first time in her life, she wished she could grab her eighteen year old self by the shoulders and shake some sense into her. 'But the worst of what they printed happened years ago. I'm not that silly little girl any more. I run my own business in London. The last picture taken outside of a nightclub was unfortunate. A reporter caught me stumbling when the heel of my shoe snapped.'

'I can't say I've seen any of the pictures, but my wife is adamant that you are a renowned party girl.'

After another sip of wine, he smiled warmly at her—the same

one he'd given her when they'd met. Her shoulders relaxed.

'But between you and me, my wife is prone to exaggerating the truth.' He winked at her before polishing off the remainder of his glass. She grinned back. 'Why don't we finish this bottle?'

'I'd love to.' The tightness in her chest evaporated and she enjoyed the rest of the afternoon with Mr Santos who insisted she call him Pablo.

The elevator doors opened. Ric took a deep breath before he stepped into the penthouse. Tonight would be the first time he'd laid eyes on Alexa since Wednesday evening and he had no idea how she'd react to him. Luckily, he'd been needed more and more at the building site and emails regarding the charity ball were the only communication that passed between them. The formal way they'd been addressing one another didn't sit well with him, but when the alternative led to him kissing her, he didn't want to stir things up. Leaving his home at the crack of dawn and returning after midnight meant he'd never had to see her, even though he felt the pull to her stronger than ever.

Ric knew he owed her an apology. He almost stripped her naked then rejected her. Where the control had come from to stop, he had no idea. The look on her face haunted him all week but he didn't know whether bringing it up again would rock the boat.

When he walked past her room, he hesitated. His hand itched to twist the knob and enter but he knew after Wednesday that he wouldn't be able to keep his hands off her if he found her less than dressed. The angry words she'd thrown at him and the talk of sleeping with other men had jealousy crashing through him and all he'd wanted to do was show her that she belonged to him, no one else.

He made his way to his own room and showered. Alexa didn't belong to him and he didn't want her to, but his primal instinct, the attraction he felt toward her mixed with the tension vibrating through the air between them had made him lose control. Something he didn't wish to do again.

Control had been his lifeline since the Castillos took him off the streets. There was a time in his late teens when he needed to feel something other than all the nothingness, and thought partying and dangerous sports were the answer. He soon realised then that adrenaline wasn't the thing he longed to feel. Years on he still hadn't figured out why he felt so empty.

Once changed, he made his way to the kitchen for a drink. Alexa perched on one of the stools by the table. A floor length purple gown encased her beautiful body. There wasn't a hint of leg or even cleavage, the dress cut across her collarbone demurely. With her wild bob tamed into smooth curls, she looked like a different woman. He swallowed.

'Hi,' she greeted him, her expression wary.

'You look...' He couldn't find the words.

She smiled. 'Sensible?'

'Beautiful.'

Alexa turned back to the steaming cup on the table. 'Thank you.' She picked up the mug and sipped.

He noticed the dress cut down her back, but not as deep as the gold one had. The teaser of bronzed skin heated his blood more than the one which exposed more of her body. He wondered why she chose this dress, one so much more conservative than the last, but thought it was better not to ask. Chances were she'd picked it so he wouldn't pounce on her again. A stab of disappointment hit him.

'Are you ready to go?'

Alexa nodded and then rose. She picked a clutch bag from the table and waited until he gestured for her to leave first. His mind whirred as he wondered what she was doing. Where had the woman gone who did what she liked when she wanted to? Where was the woman who irritated him so much he wanted to strangle her? And got him so hot he kissed her like an animal, even pushed her up against metal surfaces?

She was quiet in the car on the way over, only offering information when asked about work or the charity ball. The air was thick with her discomfort, and he wanted more than anything to take it away. Since he'd opted to drive rather than have his driver take them, he couldn't read her face properly.

Ric escorted her into the club. It was notoriously a club for rich men to drink scotch and smoke cigars, but tonight they held one of their rare events when wives were permitted to join their husbands and the chat extended further than acquisitions, shares or the economy.

He remembered Antonio bringing him years ago and the feeling he didn't quite fit in hadn't left with time. Everyone there then and now came from old money. Ric didn't know what he came from, but he doubted he'd be greeted with warm welcomes if they knew what he'd done before the Castillos had taken him in.

By the time he'd introduced Alexa to a dozen or so couples, he wondered where she had disappeared to. The woman he knew had been replaced with a polite, warm stranger who was the pinnacle of class. Coupled with the dress and her family name, she fitted in. If it wasn't for the stiff muscles in her back and the discomfort she still exuded, Ric would have sworn she was a different person.

He remembered the first time they'd met, when she'd told him her father dragged her to functions like this all the time. He could tell then she'd hated them, maybe even hated her father a little for it and he wished he could understand why. Maybe then he could understand why she acted differently tonight than she had at the first function.

When Mr Santos crossed the room without his wife and beamed

at Alexa, Ric's suspicions rose.

'Alexa, how lovely to see you.'

She offered her hand to him. 'Pablo, the pleasure's all mine.'

Pablo? When had she started calling him that?

'And Ric, always a pleasure. You should come here more often.'

Stumped, Ric shook Santos' extended hand. He eyed Alexa for an explanation but she looked away so quickly he wondered if he'd imagined the guilt in her expression. His stomach took a dive.

'Alexa's told me all about the ball you're hosting Ric, and I have to say I'm impressed with the attendance you've managed to secure. Most couples here tonight will come solely for the networking opportunities and I'm sure you will be able to squeeze a lot from their wallets for your charity.'

Ric gaped at Santos. *What had Alexa done?*

'My father and his associates are looking forward to making your acquaintance,' Alexa told the old man.

To anyone else, she appeared to be simply stating a fact. If every muscle hadn't tensed under his palm, Ric might have believed her father's attendance didn't worry her.

'He must be extremely proud to have a daughter like you,' Santos added.

Her shoulder's stiffened but she smiled warmly.

'I'll let you two mingle,' Santos said. 'I'll see you soon, *novio*. Ric.'

He nodded farewell to the older man then turned to Alexa. She looked around the room, everywhere but directly at him.

'Come.' He steered her toward an empty table and held out a chair.

She slid into it, never meeting his gaze. 'Thank you.'

Ric took the seat across from her, forcing her to look at him. 'Dare I ask how you pulled that off?' He was half-joking but he was obviously missing something important.

Alexa swallowed, only increasing his unease. 'I asked him to

103

meet me this afternoon so I could apologise. Show him I wasn't the girl the media loves to paint as the wild child.'

'And he just believed you?'

Her eyes blazed and he caught a glimpse of the Alexa he knew beneath the polished facade. Ric smiled.

'Yes,' she ground out through clenched teeth. 'Because that's not who I am any more.'

Ric almost laughed. She was still wild; a fancy dress and her demure appearance wouldn't change that. But he didn't. He remembered the first night he caught her coming back with her friends. She hadn't been drunk, not even giddy. And again when he found her with Daniel outside Beaches. She had switched to water and sobered up by the time he reached her. Maybe she had grown up and maybe the media did exaggerate for the most part.

Ric decided to change the subject. 'Why did you invite your father?'

Her whole body froze before him and her expression shuttered. 'He has friends in high places.' She shrugged, the movement too jerky to be blasé.

'Why don't you get along with him?'

A woman hired for the evening began to sing in a quiet under-tone, relaxing the atmosphere, but it did nothing to ease the built up tension in Alexa. She didn't answer for a long moment and he wondered if she would when the second verse of the song began.

'He sees me as something he owns. A pretty face to have on his arm after my mother died.' Alexa stared at the table. 'He wants me to marry into money, into class. He wants me to marry a man like him, but I won't. I don't want to end up like my mother. I'd rather be single and free.'

Understanding dawned and his chest swelled painfully. Her father used her, just as Ric had allowed himself to be used through his teenage years. Now he could understand her rebellion, the

104

refusal to do what was asked of her if it wasn't something she wanted to do.

He realised with horror that he was doing exactly the same. He'd given her no choice and was using her to help organise the ball. How could she ask her father and his friends to come after the way Ric treated her? It seemed now he had two things to make up for.

'Ric, dear,' his adopted mother, Maria placed a hand on his shoulder, halting his questions.

Alexa lifted her gaze to smile at the woman.

'Hello, Alexa.' She slid into the chair next to Ric.

He forced himself to smile at Maria as Alexa had. It wasn't easy, not when the only person who knew the things he'd done, the things he'd had to do to survive, still looked at him without any disgust whatsoever.

'I wanted to say hello before you disappeared, I know you don't like these events.' She placed a hand on his arm. His chest warmed at the touch and the fact she spoke in English in case Alexa couldn't speak their tongue made his smile more real.

'No, I don't.'

Maria's eyes filled with compassion and he felt Alexa's gaze burn a hole in the side of his head.

'A beautiful girlfriend deserves to be taken out more often. You should bring Alexa over for dinner.'

His eyes widened at her assumption, but before he could correct Maria, Alexa beat him to it. 'Ric and I aren't involved, Mrs Castillo.'

'Alexa is helping me organise the ball at the end of the month,' he added.

Maria studied his face. She shook her head, a smile curved her lips. She said in Spanish, 'You can't fool an old fool.'

He opened his mouth to insist she had it wrong but she gave him a look that said she could see right through him, and maybe she could. Whatever pulled him toward Alexa had only grown stronger the last few days.

Maria rose and kissed his cheek. 'I'll let you two sneak away now.' After bidding Alexa a warm goodnight and throwing Ric an expectant look, she left them.

Alexa's gaze focused intently on his face. 'Why does she make you so uncomfortable?'

She watched as every muscle in his body tensed beneath the penguin suit. His face morphed into an emotionless mask. Maybe she'd pushed him too far with the question, but if he was going to make her talk about Robert the least he could do was give a little back.

'Instead of thanking them for adopting me, I wasted my allowance on wild nights out and as many dangerous sports as I could.'

'That's why you work so hard for them. You feel like you let them down.' She could understand that. After all, she'd let her father down more than once.

Ric frowned. 'I think we've spoken to everyone we need to. Let's go.'

Her curiosity burned but she let him escort her out of the club. He'd said his life was none of her business. On the way back to the hotel, Alexa wondered why he couldn't see that it didn't matter to Maria what he did. After all, he was making up for his mistakes now and Maria obviously cared about him. Love had filled her eyes as soon as she'd looked at Ric.

Back at the penthouse, Ric walked straight to the kitchen and she heard the familiar thud of a bottle hitting the counter. She went to her room, intent on letting it go, but she couldn't ignore the sound of his pained sigh and her feet carried her through to him.

With his broad back to her, his hands rested on the counter and he stared at the glass in front of him. Her heart thudded painfully. She crossed the room and went to reach out but lowered her hand before she could touch him. He'd rejected her already. If he pulled away now, she was sure she'd form that complex.

Alexa swallowed against the lump of emotion lodged in her throat. 'Are you going to drink all that yourself?'

He turned, half his mouth curved and he silently handed her his glass. He pulled another from the cupboard and filled it with whiskey. She didn't drink the stuff, it always burned her throat, but after tonight she knew the tension in her body and the discomfort she felt at the party wouldn't be cured by a hot bath or a good night's sleep. Nor would the dread of having her father in Spain, judging and assessing her every move and taking control of her.

She slid onto one of the stools, took a sip of the fiery liquid and made a face as it burned her throat on the way down.

Ric laughed. 'It's an acquired taste.' He joined her at the table and set his glass down next to hers. 'But helps when there are things you want to forget about.' He circled the rim with his forefinger, his gaze fixed on the brown liquid.

'Alcohol isn't the answer.' She'd learned that in her late teens. It made her father angry, not attentive or loving. Alexa doubted anything would.

He chuckled again, but it sounded forced. 'I never thought you would be the one to lecture me on alcohol.'

The words should have offended her, but when he looked up she saw the smile he wore hadn't reached his eyes. They were open now, showing the pain he'd suffered and she wished she could take it away.

He ran a hand through his hair and then downed the last of the whiskey in his glass. The pain fled his expression so quickly Alexa wondered if she'd imagined it, but she knew she hadn't. He was just good at hiding it.

'I suppose we better have an early night if we want to beat the traffic in the morning.'

She didn't have a clue what he was on about. 'The morning?'

His smile this time warmed his eyes and made her long for melted chocolate. 'I never back out of a bet.'

With that, he left her perched at the table, gaping at his retreating form. She'd forgotten about the bet and was shocked he was paying his dues. There'd been so much to do this week, between organising the party, keeping up with her role as his PA and her own business, she didn't realise how stressed she truly was until he'd mentioned the trip to Water World. A spark of giddy excitement lightened her mood instantly. Tomorrow she'd show Ric the fun he'd missed out on when he was young.

Chapter Nine

'Ric you'd think it was hell I dragged you to, not a water park.'

Alexa pulled open a locker and stuffed the huge beach bag into it. She'd packed the thing this morning with so much stuff, Ric wondered what she'd need it all for. She grabbed a bottle of sun cream and a pair of shades.

He frowned at her back. 'It's far too early in the morning to listen to children screaming.' Surely there was a better way to make it up to her than this.

Giggling, she slid off her robe exposing bronze skin everywhere. Ric knew when she'd appeared in the lime string bikini this morning that today was going to be a test of his self-control. His gaze dipped down to her curved bottom and heat shot straight to his groin, making his water-proof shorts a little tight.

She slipped the shades on and turned to face him. Ric snapped his gaze to her face. 'You'll get used to it.'

'Maybe after coffee.'

She shook her head and pointed to his t-shirt. 'Off.'

Ric pulled the t-shirt over his head and handed it to her. Without hesitating or gawking, she took the shirt and turned back to the locker. He frowned at her back as his body cooled off.

It heated straight back up again when she walked over to a bench and began creaming herself up with sun lotion. When she bent her arms awkwardly to reach her back, he crossed the dry grass.

'Give me the cream before you hurt yourself.'

Alexa turned, her eyebrows rose above the metallic glasses. 'Okay.'

She handed him the bottle. He squirted some cream on his palm and rubbed his hands together, praying his body would behave. She shivered as he spread the cream over her back and he made sure he covered every inch. Her skin was silky and firm. He gritted his teeth and pretended he couldn't hear her soft moan when his hands reached her shoulder blades.

'All done.'

He handed back the cream and turned around, wishing he had glasses to hide the lust he knew would be shining from his eyes. The mountain in the centre of the park had slides and tubes protruding from different levels all the way up. Shallow looking pools surrounded the base. He really should have thought of another way to apologise for his behaviour.

Alexa's hand touched his back and he sucked in a breath.

'You'll burn if you don't wear any.'

He nodded. If he weren't so aware of her soft, surprisingly firm hands on him he might have missed the fact they were shaking. His lips pulled up at the corners and the last of the tension drained from his body. At least he wasn't the only one suffering this crazy attraction. But that couldn't be a good thing. Alexa's family name worked wonders in securing a great guest list, but he was still worried what would happen if the media thought they were dating. He'd made sure to tell everyone so far that they were only business partners.

Her hands froze at his left shoulder and he knew what had caught her attention. He turned around. 'Let's get this over with.'

Even though the sunglasses hid her eyes, he felt them burning into him with curiosity. But he didn't want to think about the scar and definitely didn't want to remember how he'd gotten it. 'I thought you were supposed to be teaching me how to have fun.'

She smiled but he wanted to see her eyes, knew they'd tell him how she really felt.

'I hope you're not scared of heights.' The smile morphed into a smirk.

Ric shook his head. '*Querida*, it would take a lot more than a high slide to scare me.'

Alexa returned the sun cream to their locker and dragged him by the hand up the stairs. His thighs burned by the time they reached the top, but the ache in his groin hurt more. With her peach-like backside bobbing up ahead of him, he hadn't been able to drag his gaze away from it. He knew, without a doubt, he could pick her bottom out from thousands.

There were two slides at the top of the hill. One enclosed and the other looked like it dropped you down a meter, then over a curve and kept going that way until it rocketed you into the shallow depths beneath. He could see children and adults flying down, screaming with laughter as they fell. His stomach dipped a notch. He didn't think it looked very safe, never mind fun.

Alexa dragged him away to the other side with the closed off tubes. They looked better. At least there was no way to fall out. A couple of boys ahead of them grabbed a black rubber ring each and when the light above the hole turned from red to green, they both jumped through one each. Their screams echoed all the way down.

'Do you want to go down by yourself, or with me?'

Alexa stood next to rings with double holes. Not even under the pain of torture would he admit he'd prefer if she was with him, so he shrugged. She paused for a second, then grabbed a double.

The man working the slide explained to them to keep their arms as close to their bodies as possible and to hold onto the handles on the rubber rings. Ric followed Alexa into the water and then sat wide legged on the back, almost toppling the thing with his weight. She grabbed her end, right between his legs and beamed at him.

'They can be a little tricky.'

He laughed. 'Next time I'll get it right.'

'If you don't have an accident in your shorts on the way down.'

Ric grinned. She slid onto the front and shuffled them over to the edge of the hole. He watched the red light, anticipation and excitement warring through him. This was much better than speedboat racing or freefalling. At least the risk of severe bodily harm was at a minimum.

The light changed to green and he gripped the side of the hole, then hauled them both into the darkness. They shot down, the only sounds he could hear were Alexa's breathy laugh and the water rushing around them. Suddenly they twisted and his weight shifted on the ring until it felt like he'd fall off. He grabbed her around the waist and she squeezed his forearms. The panic inside him dissipated as they dropped again and it felt like his stomach would burst out of his head.

Ric laughed, unable to help himself as they swayed from side to side, were thrown around corners then finally shot out of the tube and into the air. They hit the water on the ring but both of them bounced off it and into the pool. When his head broke the surface, he looked around for Alexa. She stood a few feet away with the ring, dripping wet with a smile that brought out his own.

'Fun?' she asked.

He nodded slightly.

'More fun than, you know?'

He worked out what she meant, but he wanted to hear her say it. He feigned a look of innocence. 'More fun than…?'

'Than…*you know*. What you told me your idea of fun was.'

He enjoyed her squirming as he neared. Leaning forward, he

hovered his lips right above her ear. 'I want to hear you say it.'

Her breath sped and her lips twisted as she backed up, kicking her feet in the pool and spraying him with water. 'Castillo, you can go purr.' But she smiled.

He grinned until she removed her glasses and he saw the lust shining from her eyes, then his smile slipped away. 'Almost.' He admitted.

'Wow. You're sleeping with the wrong women then.' She slipped her glasses back on. A cheeky smile curved her lips. 'We have to take this over there.' She pointed to a stand with other rubber rings and then waded through the water toward it.

He followed, wishing he hadn't tried to tease her. Now he craved a different kind of fun with the heiress and although he thought she wanted the same thing, it was better they kept their relationship professional. At least that's what he kept trying to convince himself.

Not only would dating Alexa be risky but he wouldn't be able to give her what she or her father wanted. He didn't have class, or the ability to love. God knows he'd tried to feel something for the Castillos but couldn't. Even now.

All he could offer Alexa was great sex for a couple of weeks, but he knew she deserved more. Still, when he was with her, he couldn't resist flirting, couldn't stop himself from wanting to be closer to her.

Maybe he should give her the choice.

Alexa wanted to leave the dipping slide until last. She was sure after that all the others would look tame, but hadn't been sure which slides Ric would go on. He surprised her by dragging her on them all, twice, even racing her down the double tubes and winning of course. She remembered his smug grin; the look he'd thrown her insinuating she'd been an idiot to assume there would be any other outcome.

As they sat on the grass eating the sandwiches she'd packed this morning, Alexa decided it was time. Her whole being throbbed with the need to wipe that cocky smile off his face. Right after she had a good look at the muscles on his chest bunching with each movement. She knew the minute he whipped off his t-shirt bringing the glasses was a good idea. Her gaze slid over his torso way too much to be normal and she dreaded to think what he'd say if he caught her at it.

The 'look, don't touch' mantra she chanted in her head wasn't stopping her hands itching to reach out.

She leaned back on her arms, looked up at the afternoon sun in the sky. The grass felt dry and almost crispy beneath her fingers. The colour was so different to back home.

'It's time to man up, Castillo.'

He raised a brow, amusement glittered in his eyes. She smiled. For all his eagerness with every other ride, he'd avoided the dipping slide all day.

'Time to go on the big boy ride.' She pointed to the top of the hill to the slide next to the tubes.

His eyes grew wary. Alexa smirked, knowing she'd been right. 'Don't tell me you're wimping out.'

'Green, I've never backed down from a challenge.' He rose and held out a hand toward her.

She reached for his hand and grabbed on. He whipped her up and circled her waist with his arms, pressed her body against his. Alexa was sure her heart was on a mission to burst out of her rib cage.

'Any challenge,' he whispered.

The look in his eyes said he meant more than going on the ride. A flamethrower must have been aimed at her because she felt her whole body burn with need. She couldn't get a breath, couldn't find the strength to push him away. Where Ric was concerned, her body seemed to bow to his will. When he released her, she sucked in a huge gulp of air.

The git grinned, knowing full well what he did to her. Irritation warred with her hormones and won.

'All talk and no action makes Ric an ass.'

She turned and stomped toward the ride, his throaty laugh igniting the needy fire inside rather than her irritation which pissed her off more.

When they reached the queue, she chanced a look over her shoulder, unable to keep her gaze off that masterpiece for long. It really wasn't fair. God should have at least given him narrow shoulders with that face. The chest just made him too hot, dangerously so.

His gaze was on her backside and she thought about calling him on it, instead she wiggled her bum. With wide eyes he snapped his attention up to her face.

'Perv,' she accused and then turned her back to him.

'Tease,' he whispered in her ear.

His hands settled on her hips and she had to fight the urge to jerk away or, worse, melt into him. She wouldn't lose this game.

'It's only teasing if I actually tried. How about knocking that ego down a notch?' She smirked over her shoulder and her breath caught at the look in his eyes.

'If you were Pinocchio you'd have had my eye out with this.' His thumb grazed her nose and she turned away from him.

'Keep telling yourself you're irresistible, Ric. Others might actually start to believe it.' Why was he still touching her? Was he trying to kill her?

'I thought all a woman wanted was a rich businessman.' His laugh was mocking and his comment gave her the strength she needed to step out from his hold.

She turned on him, anger seeping into her tone. 'There's more to life than money, Ric.'

Understanding softened his face. 'Alexa, I didn't mean—'

'Forget it.' She couldn't believe she'd told Ric anything about her father and what kind of man he wanted for her. She turned her back on him and moved along with the queue. 'Money isn't what I want.'

She watched couples and children shoot down the slide as they crept nearer to the top. Ric remained silent behind her but she refused to turn around. Why couldn't he just insult her, tell her money was all she seemed to care about or something? Being pissed off at him was better than feeling pitied.

Their turn arrived and Alexa stepped into the shallow pool with two others. Ric followed at her side. The water rushed over the edge and adrenaline sped through her veins like a drug. Excitement bubbled and she turned to him, a grin splitting her face.

He eyed the drop warily, all trace of teasing and pity gone.

'Wimp.'

Determination shone from every rigid angle of his face and he sat on the edge of the slide. He looked up at her. 'Don't tell me you're backing out, Green.'

She settled onto the slide next to him. 'Not a chance, Castillo. I wouldn't miss hearing you scream like a little girl for anything. Even new shoes.'

'Go.' The man working the slide shouted.

Alexa let go of the sides and the current of water under her bum pulled her down. The drop was almost vertical and when she shot over the edge it felt like she was falling. She laughed, the adrenaline raging and making her feel giddy, high even. When she hit the first curve she almost spun around but managed to right herself before the next drop.

Her heart thundered in her chest, a grin split her cheeks and she couldn't hear anything over the slosh of the water and her own laughter. On the last dip her body spun and she shot backward into the shallow pool. The force pulled her under and when she burst her head through the water gasping and laughing, Ric smirked at her from a few feet away. His chest glistened brown and shiny.

'Missing something?'

He held up a pair of lime-green bikini bottoms and Alexa's hands flew to her bare hips under the water.

'Gimme.' She held her hand out, using the other to cover her modesty. She darted a glance nervously around before returning her gaze to him with a scowl. 'Now, Castillo. This isn't funny.'

He grinned. 'Come and get them.' He backed into shallow water, a twinkle in those infuriating eyes.

'I'm going to kill you and I'm going to enjoy it. Get the knickers over here. Now!'

She stood her ground, removed her glasses and threw him her best don't-mess-with-me-Castillo glare.

The amusement softening his face said he enjoyed her embarrassment profusely. She would kill him. And she'd enjoy that.

He stepped toward her as more bodies shot from the slide and splashed her with water. He didn't hand them to her until he was close enough to see her hands beneath the water. Alexa grabbed the knickers, turned her back to him and quickly pulled them on. When she turned around, she saw him jerk his gaze away from the water.

'Pervert,' she accused again.

Ric grinned. 'Alexa, I doubt there's any man on Earth who could resist looking.'

She knew he was teasing her, but it made her all too aware of the fact that he'd rejected her. Her good mood took a nose dive and she tried to keep hold of the irritation of him pinching her knickers. Alexa stormed out of the pool toward the locker room, intent on calling it a day. Removing the key from the band on her wrist, she pulled the door open with such force it slammed into the other door.

'Glad to see it's not just my office you wreck with doors.' The smug tone he used hit all the wrong buttons.

She whirled on him. 'That wasn't funny.'

He backed her up against the lockers with his body, the black sun tattoo right in her face. Every shred of irritation fell away and loopy hormone juice seeped to every part of her.

His hands circled her waist, his fingers grazed the top of her buttocks and she daren't move. If he slid his hands lower, pulled her closer, she'd be lost in lust. Alexa fought the urge to touch him.

Ric shook his head then dipped so his lips were a flick of a tongue away from hers. 'It was a little, admit it. Anyway, wasn't it you who said I needed to lighten up?' His hot breath brushed across her face and froze her tongue. 'I think you should listen to your own advice.'

The lust darkening his eyes made her think he wanted to kiss her but he didn't move forward and to hell if she would. In that second she wanted it, because this Ric wasn't the kind of man her father would approve of. Nonsense was the lowest of the low on the list of qualities he looked for in associates and nonsense was all she got from Ric today. She'd take the hit. This time.

'It was embarrassing,' she admitted, because with his hard body pressed against hers, his hot breath on her face and her body throbbing for him, she couldn't lie. Still, she wasn't going to admit it was his comment about not being able to resist looking at her body that embarrassed her more.

'I didn't mean to, *querida*. I'm sorry.' Sincerity shone from those melted irises and she couldn't doubt him. 'Do you want to leave, or do you want to go on that one again?'

His wicked grin gave her the strength to push him away but

she smiled now she could breathe again. 'How about another race on the tubes?'

'You never learn.' He shook his head in faux disappointment. 'What does the winner get?'

A kiss almost slipped out but she caught herself in time. He eyed her suspiciously, but she thought on her feet. 'The loser has to make dinner tonight.'

'Then I hope you can cook.' He winked.

'No need to worry about my culinary skills. It will be you slaving over the stove when we get back.'

'We'll see,' he said with an I-can't-believe-you-haven't-learned-by-now look on his face.

'You're going down, Castillo.'

Chapter Ten

Losing once? Shame on her. Three times took the biscuit.

Alexa flipped the spiced chicken in the pan and cursed Ric. He'd reminded her of a kindred spirit, all happy and light as she'd rushed to keep up with him and lost race after stinking race. Her legs would be sore tomorrow from climbing the stairs all day. Still, it was worth it to see the stressed businessman take a day off and enjoy himself, even if it meant she'd have to pay her dues.

'That smells amazing.'

Alexa turned to see him standing in the doorway of the kitchen, a white fluffy towel around his waist and that chest still damp from his shower. God, it had almost killed her today. The black outline of a burning sun over his right pec still made her mouth water. Couldn't he just dress for dinner like any normal person? She caught the amusement in his eyes. Well, if he wanted to play that game... Alexa slipped off her robe so she was left in her bikini.

She turned back to the stove and stirred the rice. 'It's Mexican, I hope you like spicy.'

His feet slapped against the marble tiles as he made his way over to her. It took every ounce of strength not to turn around and gape at him. She had no glasses to hide behind now and after his smug victories, she wouldn't give him the satisfaction.

'It looks great. I'm glad you're able to pay your penance.'

Her blood sizzled. Alexa swallowed. 'I don't back out on a bet either.'

Or crazy dares. Or anything once she'd been goaded into it.

The fridge clinked open and he pulled out a bottle of wine. She sneaked a peak at his broad, hard back and her tummy quivered. The long, white scar on his right shoulder made her heart throb. It took everything she had that morning not to ask him how he'd got that scar. She turned back to the stove and her mind whirred with the awful possibilities. She forgot her vow to make him pay.

Ric set the table while she finished cooking. After dishing the food onto the plates, she carried them over to him. He filled two glasses with wine and after she'd settled into a chair, he got to work on devouring the food.

'You have to teach my chef how to make this.' He popped a forkful of pilau rice and spicy chicken into his mouth and groaned.

The sound resonated in her tummy and sparked a slow burning fire between her thighs. It didn't help that he hadn't bothered to dress. She did her best to keep her attention on her plate, pushing the rice around with her fork. Wondering what he'd suffered in the past made her stomach queasy.

'Aren't you hungry?'

She looked up to see him study her over the rim of his glass. He swallowed and she watched his Adam's apple bob. After seeing another side of him at the water park, she'd begun to forget what kind of a man he was and she'd realised that even through the goading and teasing, he didn't have a stick up his ass all the time. Jumping his bones seemed like a better idea by the second but she knew he didn't really want that and after all she'd learned about him, shared with him, she didn't think she'd be able to handle the rejection.

'Starving,' she lied.

She scooped up a forkful and popped it in her mouth. After

chewing methodically, she reached for the wine and took a long gulp, wishing her hands would stop shaking. Her body felt wound too tight, like it had the other day when he'd kissed her. Like it had today every time he touched her. She remembered being on the boat, in his arms, then pressed against the fridge, his hard body pinning her there, and her knees had almost given out. And today, when he'd had her trapped between his sodding chest and the lockers. She shuddered.

Ric eyed her over the rim of his glass, humour and something dark heating his gaze. It was too much. She needed an ice bath before she overheated. Picking up the still full plate, she rose.

'Actually, I'm not that hungry.'

She made it to the sink and scraped her plate, but when she tried to rinse it under the tap, Ric's hand snared her wrist. His breath hot against her neck, the heat of his naked chest dangerous against her back.

'Put down the plate.'

Alexa obeyed, unable to speak or protest. Her brain seemed to have forgotten how to form words.

'Turn around.'

She did as she was asked and closed her eyes so she didn't do something stupid, like lean forward and lick his tattoo, or maybe suck one of those brown nipples into her mouth. Blood pulsed between her thighs and she squeezed them together.

His hand tilted her chin and she didn't know who was shaking, but someone definitely was.

'Open your eyes.'

She did and immediately wished she hadn't. His chocolate eyes were so dark they looked almost black, smooth jaw stiff with tension and his lips looked full and firm—as firm as they had the last time they'd stood in the kitchen and he'd taken her ability to stand away just from pressing his mouth to hers.

'I think it's time we stopped lying to ourselves.'

Her lips parted as she gasped. His thumb skimmed her lower lip. 'What do you mean?' Her chest rose and fell with her need, her desire, but fear kept her sane. Fear was good.

'I want you, and you want me.'

'I don't want to,' she admitted.

'And I don't want to either.'

She knew that, had always known. So why did it feel like a sucker punch to her stomach?

'But it doesn't change the fact that we do.' His eyes grew serious as he released her chin. 'This can't be more than sex and we'd have to be discreet.'

His expression pleaded with her to understand, but she couldn't. Why did he care if the world knew they were having an affair? Then she remembered. He was all about respect. The stick-in-his-ass Ric thought he was too good for her.

The realisation worked quicker than the ice bath. 'No.' She moved around him, then toward the door. He caught her by the wrist and her anger spiked. She turned to him with her best scowl. 'I said, *no.*'

'I heard you. Now I want you to tell me why.'

She ground her teeth, managed not to stomp her foot or let go of the irritated shriek lodged in her throat. 'I refuse to sleep with someone who's ashamed of me.'

Ric's eyes widened. 'I'm not ashamed of you. Why would you think that?'

She studied his expression, looking for a hint he was lying and coming up empty. 'Then why do you want to keep it discreet?'

He let go of her and the shutters slammed down on his expression, then he walked over to the table and took a long draw of the wine. Alexa watched his eyes shut, his chest heave as he inhaled and wondered what the heck was so bad he couldn't tell her without alcohol.

'The British media still follow you around. Perhaps not in Spain, but if word got out that we were together, they'd dig into my past and I'd rather it stayed buried.'

Her chest tightened and she struggled to breathe. What horrors had he faced and why would he be ashamed of them? Unwelcome images of Ric as a young boy, frightened, cold and alone entered her mind and she couldn't shake them free. Her throat sucked closed and tears stung her eyes.

Ric turned to her, his expression carefully blank. Alexa wished she could do that—hide everything from everyone, but she couldn't find the strength.

'I'm not available long-term, Alexa. I don't want love or commitment.'

Heat licked her belly as pain for what he'd had to endure tortured her from the inside out. She'd seen a different side of him today, one he probably didn't know existed and she wanted to see more of that man—however much he annoyed her—but knew it was impossible. The fact that the controlling, arrogant businessman was still in him should be enough of a libido killer, but it hadn't been. In fact, the more time passed the more she forgot why she should back away.

But the thing that scared her the most was ending up tied down in a relationship with a man who saw her as a possession. A tool to do his bidding and a beauty at his side. Ric didn't want any of that. He wanted to have sex with her and she'd grow a twenty inch nose if she said she didn't want that too.

'Not tonight,' she said.

He cocked a brow and leaned his hip against the table. 'What's wrong with tonight?'

The teasing glint in his eye made her wish she had a better reason than she did. If she slept with him now, with her emotions all over the place, she didn't know what would happen. Better to wait until she regrouped.

But she wouldn't tell him that, instead she went with another excuse. She forced a grin onto her face. 'Call it payback for pinching my knickers.'

He didn't laugh like she'd expected him to. Instead he strode toward her, all intense with a gleam in his eye that said he'd get his way. She backed up a step.

'You don't mean that. What are you hiding Alexa?'

Damn. 'What do you mean? Can't a girl dish out a little comeuppance?'

His hand cupped her cheek and her resolve pulled on a pair of running shoes. 'There's another reason you're not telling me.'

How could he do that? 'Mind reading isn't sexy.'

He laughed then. She backed away another step and he shook his head. 'I'll find out one way or the other. Tell me.'

'How did you get that scar?' she asked before she could stop herself.

His eyebrows shot up and he looked at her funny, like he was shocked that could stop her from going to bed with him. But if he got the scar from something silly, like falling out of a tree when he'd been playing with his friends, it wouldn't play on her mind so much. If he'd been hurt as a boy, her heart would hurt for him and jumping into bed with him would be a bad idea.

'What does it matter?' he asked, his voice rough. His whole torso seemed rigid and his expression closed off. Her tummy dipped. God, it was bad. 'I told you this was about attraction, nothing else.'

He did, and the words still hurt. 'It matters to me.'

'If you want to start digging into dirty laundry, there are a few things you could tell me.'

Her eyes widened and the change of direction left her head spinning. 'Like what?'

'Like why you asked your father to come when it's clear you can't stand him. Like why you've avoided growing up or settling down. Don't all women dream of a white wedding and walking down the aisle to marry a respectable man? You could have your pick.'

Alexa gritted her teeth and planted a hand on her hip. 'That's none of your bloody business.'

'Exactly.' He closed the distance between them and hauled her close by the hips. Her breasts butted off his chest. 'Now enough talking.'

His mouth came down on hers and her mind went blank. This wasn't the kind of desperate, bruising kiss he'd given her the last time they'd been in his kitchen. His lips moved with slow deliberation, trapping her swollen bottom one and sucking it into his mouth.

Her lips parted and he swept his tongue into her mouth, stroking a firm hand up her spine and knotting it into the hair at her nape. Alexa's mind disconnected from her body and she couldn't concentrate on anything except his skilled kiss. Without permission, her hands planted themselves on either side of his hips and slid up, over the hard abs, firm pecs and her fingers traced the circle of his tattoo from memory. It was smooth, like the rest of him and suddenly touch didn't feel like enough.

He picked her up and, without breaking the slow, heated kiss, took her over to the counter and set her down on top of it. Pulling away, his gaze swept down over her body, still clad in the lime bikini.

Linking his fingers into the waistband of her knickers, he winked. 'Lift your bottom.'

Her breathing sped to match her heartbeats and she obeyed, a fresh jolt of desire zapping down between her thighs. Ric dropped to her knees and removed her briefs. His gaze was level with a part of her she'd never expected him to see and she held her breath, waiting for his rejection like he did the last time they'd frisked it up in the kitchen.

'Oh god, Alexa.'

He nibbled and kissed his way from her knee to her inner thigh and her breath rushed out when he closed in on her centre. She parted her legs wider, not caring any more if he pulled away, she was pretty sure she'd drag him back by the hair. But he didn't kiss her where she needed him to. Instead, he moved to her other knee and began the same circuit. She huffed out a protest and he laughed against her thigh.

'We have all night. There's no rush.'

'I'm going to explode on my own if you don't hurry.' She bit her lip, cursing her wayward tongue.

'I'd like to see that.' His dark eyes shone with humour, but his tight jaw made her think he was as ready to burst as she was. 'But not tonight.'

His hands slid under her bottom and he squeezed, pulled her toward the edge and she yelped. She grabbed hold of the handles on the cupboards behind her and held on tight. He leaned in and her breath whooshed out in a rush. Still, he didn't touch, only inhaled, shuddered and planted a soft kiss below her belly button.

Alexa hadn't been lying about exploding; her whole body felt like one breath in the right place would do it. But he just licked his way down, then kissed the flesh on her tingling thighs.

Damn him. 'Are you waiting for an invitation?'

His nose skimmed her naked flesh next to her bikini line. 'No, I'm waiting until you're so ready, you'll come the second I taste you, then I'll make you come again and again.'

Her whole body zinged. 'Got news for you Ric, I've been there for ages.'

A smug smile curved his lips just before he leaned in and sucked her into his mouth. All the heat, the pressure in her body flooded to that point and then exploded, drawing a wordless cry from her lips and shudders from every inch of her.

He didn't ease upon that sensitive area, making her wish she could speak and tell him to back off as pain mingled with pleasure. His tongue swirled, his finger found its way inside her and he zeroed in on the spot most men thought was a myth. Ric obviously didn't, because he worked it like he had the instruction manual for her orgasms memorised.

She panted, squirmed and felt the pressure build higher, tighter until it weighed her down. Every time it built to the peak, he shifted the pressure outside and in until it she wanted to scream. After the third time, Alexa was ready to clobber him, but then he used his finger harder, sucked her into his mouth and the pressure shattered. Body melting, mind blank and seeing white, she shuddered.

He stood, facing her with glistening lips, a wry smile and come-to-bed eyes. Alexa didn't think she could move if she wanted to. She could see his erection tenting the towel and couldn't drag her gaze away from the huge peak. The first shred of unease cracked through her afterglow. It had been ages since she'd been with a man.

His hand cupped her cheek and tilted her head up. He frowned at her. 'What's wrong?' She gulped and he grinned. 'I'm not an animal, *querida*. It will be mind-blowing, I promise.'

He dropped a sweet kiss on her lips. 'Bedroom.'

She released her death grip on the cabinets and held onto his shoulders while she slid off the counter. Her legs wobbled and Ric steadied her with an arm around her waist, grinning at her like the smug git he was.

'Pleased with yourself?' The fact he could make her irritated and want to jump his bones at the same time must be a skill he'd acquired over the years.

'Very.' He snared her hand and pulled her toward the door.

The sound of the lift clattering to life made them pause. 'Who has a key?' she asked, her heart stuttering to a halt. She was sure he'd locked it when they got back.

His whole frame stiffened and he turned to her. After looking her up and down, he said, 'Get the bottoms.'

She scuttled back to the counter, whipped up the bikini bottoms and the robe, then pulled them on. The elevator doors opened and a female voice called his name. Alexa's stomach fell to her feet and she had to put a hand on the counter for support while jealously burned through her veins. He was seeing someone, and she should be angry, she should pick up the dirty pan she'd cooked the chicken in and launch it at him, but instead her eyes burned with bloody tears.

He called something back in Spanish, then looked down at his towel, whispering something under his breath. He loosened and retied the cotton, disguising it a bit, but a shift in the wrong direction and the cheating bastard would be caught.

'Stay here,' he whispered as he ducked out of the kitchen.

She considered his command for three seconds, then stormed through to the lounge. Mrs Castillo beamed at him from the opposite side of the sofa and Alexa knew that this was the moment in her life that would have rocketed straight off the blush scale into what-the-hell-were-you-thinking territory.

Mrs Castillo turned to her. 'Alexa, what a lovely surprise.' She threw Ric a knowing smile. 'I'm sorry to intrude. I didn't know you had company.'

'Alexa is staying with me until I can find her another room. We're overbooked.' He threw Alexa a questioning look.

The older woman didn't look convinced, and if Alexa looked like she'd just had two of the most spectacular orgasms of her life, she couldn't blame her.

'We're having a barbeque tomorrow and would like you to come. I thought I'd stop by and ask you since I was passing anyway. You too, Alexa.' Mrs Castillo winked at her and Alexa smiled back.

'We have work to do for the ball.'

Her eyes widened at his brazen lie. Well, she wasn't working on a Sunday. She could feel the beach calling her.

Mrs Castillo looked between the two of them. 'It doesn't start until six.' Ric's expression said it didn't matter what time. He wouldn't back down. 'Maybe another time.'

Ric nodded and walked her over to the lift. Alexa said goodbye and waited until the doors closed until she spoke. 'Why did you lie to her?'

Raking a hand through his hair, he wondered if kissing Alexa would make the questions shining from her eyes fade. He could ease her through to his bedroom and get lost in the sweet taste of her for the rest of the night. Heat stirred beneath the towel, but he knew she wouldn't back down this time.

With her hand on her hip and a scowl marring her pretty, freshly flushed face, there was no escape he could see. But that didn't mean he'd tell her the whole truth, the reasons why he'd never accepted an invitation to his parent's home for years. 'I didn't. We have a lot still to do.'

'You do know tomorrow is Sunday?'

'This isn't a Monday to Friday job, Alexa.' He walked closer to her, an eyebrow raised. 'Now, where were we?'

The storm in her eyes shifted and her breathing sped. 'But—'

Ric pinched her lips together. 'No buts. Not this time.' He replaced his fingers with his mouth.

The soft cry at the back of her throat sent his erection from interested to impatient. Pulling her flush against him, he squeezed that firm, peachy bottom and lifted her off her feet. Alexa wrapped her legs around him. He carried her down the hall, slipping the robe from her shoulders, and set her down on the middle of her bed.

'Naked,' he managed through his ragged breathing.

130

She looked around her room, a dazed expression in her eyes. 'Why here?'

'Why not?' he countered, wondering if she'd ever just go along with him instead of challenging him at every step.

'Condoms.' He stared at her with a raised brow. 'I don't have any.'

He calculated how long it would take to run to his room, grab a pack and get back. *Too long*. He grabbed her hand and dragged her through to his bedroom. He threw the door open, released her then headed to the bedside cabinet.

Alexa eyed the box he removed from the half-filled drawer. 'That's some prep, Ric.'

He smiled. 'Better to be safe than sorry.' Tossing the box on the bed, he unhooked the towel and let it fall to the floor. Her gaze dropped and her mouth fell open. 'You're still overdressed.'

Swallowing, she reached around to unhook the clasp on the lime bikini top. She ripped her attention away from his body and stared at him with wide eyes. His chest tightened and he realised he had to slow down, not scare her away.

'Come here.'

He pulled the top down her arms and tugged her close. Ignoring the twin peaks poking into his chest, he slid his hands over her back, reassuring, comforting. She melted closer, and his erection pulsed against her stomach.

'Trust me.'

She looked up at him and he could see the trust there, see the emotion glistening in her eyes. The pull in his chest intensified, almost knocked the breath out of him and he couldn't explain what it was—he hadn't experienced anything like it before.

Maybe she was innocent, maybe she hadn't been with the bad-boy types she'd been pictured with, but Ric didn't think that was it. She hadn't been shy last week when he'd stripped her top off, hadn't been meek when he'd had her on the kitchen counter.

131

Shaking the thoughts away, he spun them around and pulled her down onto the bed with him.

Alexa shoved at his shoulders and he fell back against the pillow. She crawled on top of him, her thighs bracketing his. Before he could ask what she was doing, her head dipped and he felt the wet heat of her tongue trailing the contours of his chest. The touch sent a fresh flow of blood to his groin.

She worked her way down his stomach, the short backcombed bob tickling his skin as she went, the scent of wild berries clogged his senses. Her lips grazed the tip of his erection and he clamped down on his stomach muscles to stop from embarrassing himself. Alexa reached for the shaft, but he hauled her up by the shoulders and rolled them so he had her trapped beneath him.

'No fair.' She gasped and pouted. 'You got to do it to me.'

Ric grinned. 'When is anything in life ever fair?'

Making sure further protests were cut off with his lips on hers, his hands got busy sliding over her silky skin, tweaking the tight rosebud nipples, drawing gasps and more soft mewls from her throat. Ric swore it was a sound he'd never want to hear when someone was in bed with him, but the sound of it coming from her made arousal rage through his being. He wanted to hear what noises she'd make when he was inside of her.

Nudging her thighs wider with his knee, he slid between her legs. He thrust his hips, rubbing against her and making them both moan. Her fingers dug into his backside, heat tingling down his spine. They needed a condom.

His hand fumbled blindly on the bed, his lips trailing kisses and nips on the silky skin on her neck. Her hips rocked up to meet his thrusts, and he was slicked with her heat, losing a little more of his mind every second it took to find the damn condoms. *Where the hell did he put them?* Unwillingly, he ripped his lips away from her. 'Alexa, wait.'

Her eyes, unfocused, were black with the same crazed lust swarming through him. 'Why?' Still challenging, even now, she dug her fingers tighter to his backside and rubbed herself against him. He shuddered.

'I can't find—'

'I'm on the pill.' Her eyes rolled back as she rocked her hips. 'Have you been tested?'

His control was shot to bits, his mind in turmoil and her wetness skimming his naked flesh with every thrust wouldn't allow him to think as rationally as he knew deep down he should. 'Yes. You?'

She nodded, another mewl slipped out of her mouth and all doubts vanished. Ric reared back and thrust into her in one quick jerk. They both gasped and stared at each other for a long second. Her body was tight around him, hot, and he'd never felt anything as amazing. Flesh and heat drawing him in, as deep as he could go. His arms shook where he hovered above her.

'Are you okay?' he asked. She was a little too snug and the frown above her brow could have been discomfort. He reared away but her legs encircled his waist and hauled him back.

'Gimme a minute.'

A minute, was she crazy?

He forced a smile and locked his jaw. Her muscles tightened around him and he groaned.

Ric felt like he'd held on forever. Her expression relaxed and she released a heavy sigh. Cupping her cheeks with his hands, he rubbed the silky skin beneath his fingers. Her face was angular, but also seemed soft. Those kiss-swollen lips made him want to nibble on them for days and the cloudy platinum eyes intensified the pull inside him.

Maybe sex would break it once and for all, maybe after tonight he wouldn't feel it any more. It not, he was certain two weeks was enough to work her out of his system.

'Okay, go,' she said, squeezing her internal muscles and rocking her hips up to meet him.

His head dipped down and he gave in to his desire, nipping and licking those kiss-swollen lips as he gently rocked into her. Their breathing was drowned out by his heartbeat pounding in his ears, her cries every time he skimmed that place deep inside her made him want to take it slower, make this last.

Lifting his head, he watched ecstasy play across her features, saw the depth of her lust shining from her eyes. But then it all went to hell and something shifted. Alexa snapped her eyes shut, but not before he caught it, the look of hope and trust that he'd seen earlier mixed with some other emotion he didn't want to see—to understand.

Her hips met his thrusts, her body so warm and welcoming that he thought pulling away would kill him, but the dread filling his stomach told him no more slow and nice. The guilt eating away at him was insane. He'd promised her nothing more, so why did he feel like the worst kind of bastard?

Ric untangled her legs from his waist and leaned back on his knees. Her eyes opened, confusion was all he could see and he almost let out a sigh of relief. Still, he lifted her bottom onto his thighs and placed her ankles against his chest. This way he kept control, this way he could stop the slow, sensual strokes and make it about their joint pleasure, nothing else.

He picked up pace, thrust in and out with quick, short movements. Her channel tightened and her thighs shook as he slid deeper, her cries morphed into groans and he watched her firm breasts bob and quiver, driving him crazy. Her eyes never opened and he had the idea that if he couldn't see her, he could make this last long enough to feel her release.

Squeezing his eyes shut, he shifted the angle of his thrusts, grabbed onto her hips and held her in place. Her body shuddered, her muscles tightened and then convulsed around him. Alexa's cry of pleasure was the last thing he registered before the heat, the pressure, drained from his stomach and shot out of him and into her.

Ric collapsed on top of her, still lodged deep inside. Alexa wrapped her legs around him, holding him in place and her fingers trailed soothing circles on his heaving back. The afterglow felt different somehow, safe, and he dimly registered that the pull inside him had only intensified, but the fog of sleep crept into his brain before it could register the emotion.

Alexa knew she was in trouble. Ric had rolled away from her hold at some point, but now his body was plastered to every inch of her back and his half-mast erection prodded her bottom. But the trouble didn't come from the sex, nope, that had been the most mind-blowing experience of her life—just like he'd promised. The trouble came from her daft heart ripping itself open when he was lodged inside her.

She hadn't hid the emotions in time, had seen the panic on his face, then his withdrawal with the shift of positions. She'd let him pull away; let him take control because she'd been terrified of falling harder than she already had. His soothing breaths in her ear made her shiver and feel comforted at the same time. If she could get out of his hold without waking him, she'd be in her own bed by now.

Ric's body tensed, the arms around her grew rigid and she thought he'd woken, thought he'd chuck her out. She held her breath and waited. A slew of Spanish came from his mouth and the tone was panicked, scared even. Turning in his arms, she watched his face and saw his frown, his rigid jaw, his fear. Was he having a nightmare? Her heart cracked open again.

Alexa held his face. 'Ric, you're dreaming. It's okay.' She stroked his jaw, massaged away the frown line creasing his brow.

135

His body relaxed and his grip loosened around her. Exhaling, she squirmed free and slipped out of the bed. Another glance at his still frame and she turned to leave. God her heart hurt way more than it should. As she made her way through to her own room, she made a promise to herself to get over this silly infatuation, the sooner the better, because it had just been about sex, nothing more.

The smell of coffee woke her from a restless sleep. Alexa rubbed her eyes, then rolled over. It still felt way too early and her legs, everything south of her navel, hurt. Something grabbed her hip and pulled her onto her back. Her eyes flew open in shock.

Ric sat on the edge of her bed, his jaw tight and his expression—as bloody usual—shuttered. She eyed the cup in his hand longingly, but the naked chest behind it distracted her.

'What are you doing?' she asked. Having sex with him didn't give him the right to wake her before the sun was up.

'It's five o'clock. Time to get up.'

Her eyes widened as she stared at him, uncomprehending. *Five? No wonder her brain was mush.*

'We have work to do.'

Alexa groaned and rolled over, squeezing her eyes shut. 'Go away.'

The bed shook with his laugh. 'I bet I could find a way to wake you up.'

His hands slid up her bared leg, all the way to the hem of the silky nightgown she wore. Her hormones zinged to life, like he'd left her body programmed to respond to his touch. But her heart throbbed out a painful beat in her chest and she rolled away from him.

'I'm up,' she said and slid off the opposite side of the bed. 'Scoot. I need to shower.'

He hadn't moved, just sat there and stared at her with disbelief.

'Shoo.' She waved her hands, but his intent gaze told her he wasn't going anywhere until he said what he wanted to. Alexa rubbed her eyes again. Sighing, she sat back down on the bed, her thigh muscles stiff. 'Spit it out, Castillo.'

'Why did you sneak back to your own room?'

She watched his face, but couldn't see any emotion, any deeper meaning to his question. Fine, if he wanted to be blasé about their night together, she could do that.

Alexa shrugged. 'You talk in your sleep.'

Panic flickered across his face before he composed himself. 'Oh? What did I say?'

If his voice hadn't been wary she'd have admitted he sounded scared, terrified even and asked him what the nightmare was about. 'I don't know, you were muttering in Spanish.'

His shoulders sagged a notch, then he looked at her with a serious expression. 'Are you really on the pill?'

'You're kidding me.' She shook her head. How dare he ask her that after she'd already told him she was. 'Isn't that something you should have checked before you went ahead and came inside me?'

Ric stood, anger hardening his jaw. 'So you lied to me?'

She stomped over to a bag on the floor, pulled out a foil packet and threw it at him. He picked up the strip and studied it. She hadn't missed a bloody day, the arrogant, assuming git. 'I wouldn't lie about that.'

She turned, headed for the en suite then paused. What was she doing? Turning back to him, she glared. 'Get out.'

He placed the strip on the bedside table. 'I had to make sure.'

His words cut her deeper than the realisation that she was falling for a man like him had. Fighting the stinging in her eyes, she forced herself to keep her expression blank. 'I said get out. It's Sunday and I've got my own work to do.'

'Alexa—'

'Don't *Alexa* me.' Anger was good. Anger kept her from the pain of his distrust. 'When I agreed to work with you, I didn't agree to weekends. I have my own company, my own work. You agreed to let me, now out.'

Fury shone from his eyes, but he turned and left. She exhaled, her anger leaving her body with the breath and pain sneaked in, catching her right in the throat. With blurry vision, she turned and headed for the shower. How she was going to manage two weeks with him when it felt like her heart would break was a mystery, but she'd come too far with the event to back out now.

And now, more than ever, Alexa wanted to change the world's opinion of her. To make her father, Ric and everyone else see that she'd changed, that she was an adult who cared about things other than herself. That would have to get her through the next fortnight. Only problem was, she wasn't sure that it would be enough.

Chapter Eleven

Ric had made a mess of things with Alexa.

He'd pushed her into admitting their attraction, been so lost in lust he hadn't stopped to make sure she was on the pill and had accused her of lying, even though deep down he knew she'd been telling the truth. Alexa said herself she didn't want marriage or kids and she wouldn't trick him like most of the women he'd been with. If Alexa wanted something, she'd tell him.

He tried to concentrate on what felt like the millionth version of the revised contract on his desk, but his mind kept flicking back to her. The pain in her eyes lodged behind her anger was harsher than a kick to the gut and he couldn't hide from his guilt.

This morning, when he'd woken alone and reached for her, felt the cold sheets on the other side of his bed, he panicked. Usually, he didn't allow women to spend the night; he hadn't ever slept next to anyone. The fact that she'd been the one to leave stung. Then to find out he had another nightmare and she witnessed it, made the last of his rational thinking take a hike. He lashed out, tried to distract them both with the accusation about the pill. It was a stupid thing to do.

He ran a hand through his hair and checked the clock. Late afternoon sun shone through the window but he still felt cold. He had to make it up to her somehow.

The penthouse was quiet except for the rhythmic tapping of keys on a laptop. He made his way to her room, paused in the doorway at the sight of her cross-legged on the middle of the bed, a Mac on her lap. He'd never seen her so focused, so serious before. The pull inside urged him forward.

She looked up, her expression blank. 'Two tics.' Her forefingers hammered the keys faster and he wondered again what her business was. 'Ok.' This time when she turned to him, she closed her laptop lid. 'What do you want?'

Ric knew he deserved that. 'Actually, I was going to ask you the same thing. I want to take you out for dinner. Your choice.'

Her brows furrowed with suspicion and again, he couldn't blame her. He'd been the one to insist they keep things discreet but having dinner with his event organiser wouldn't rock the boat. Keeping his hands to himself shouldn't be a problem because after this morning he wasn't sure that she would want him to touch her anyway.

'Anywhere I want?' she asked.

Ric nodded.

'No arguments?'

'No arguments,' he agreed, regretting it immediately. But if she wanted to drag him to a fast food place to punish him, he'd man up and eat it.

'Ok.' She slid from the bed and walked over to the suitcases by the wardrobes.

He frowned. 'Haven't you unpacked yet?'

With her back to him, she shook her head. 'What's the point when a room could become free? I don't want to have to unpack to have to pack again. I hate packing.'

'You don't have to move.'

Her fingers froze on the zip. 'I'd prefer to have my own space.'

She was still mad at him, why else would she insist on leaving?

'You have your own space here. I thought we were…' What could he say? Together? They weren't, not really.

'Sleeping together?' Looking over her shoulder, she pursed her lips. 'A one night stand doesn't change anything.'

'It wasn't a one night stand.' Where was this coming from? 'Alexa, I thought we agreed not to lie to ourselves any more.'

She turned back to the suitcase and unzipped it. 'That was before I knew you didn't trust me.'

He crossed the room, picked her up and turned her around to face him. She struggled in his hold, but he didn't let go. 'That was a mistake. I shouldn't have said that.'

She tilted her chin and he let her see his sincerity, but she didn't look convinced. Sighing, he cupped her cheek and touched his forehead to hers. 'I'd like you to stay with me.' Their hearts seemed to beat as one and he held his breath, waiting for her to speak.

'Ok,' she said at last.

Ric didn't realise his body had been tensed as if for an onslaught until his shoulders sagged with relief. He dropped a quick kiss to her nose, threaded his fingers into her hair and looked down at her with a smile. A quick round of make-up sex before dinner sounded like a good idea.

Last night, when he'd thought he saw emotion burning in her eyes, it had terrified him, but the more he'd thought about it, the more he realised that was probably wishful thinking on his part. He didn't want her to fall for him, but to be cared about would be different.

She wasn't with him for his money or false pretences; she had been in his bed because she was attracted to him, pure and simple. And he wanted her just as much.

'I want to go to Maria's barbeque.'

He released her and stepped back like her words took a swing at him. Alexa's eyes widened as she studied his reaction. Pulling himself together, he frowned at her. 'No.'

Steely eyes met his with challenge. 'You said we could go anywhere I want. I want to go to the barbeque.'

Guilt crept through the shock in his body, but it wasn't powerful enough to mask the ice in his veins. 'No. I'll take you anywhere else. Even that horrid bar on the beach if that's what you want.'

She eyed him thoughtfully and he could almost see her brain ticking over. 'Fine, we'll go somewhere else if you tell me why you won't go to the Castillos'.'

Ric swallowed but he wasn't going to back down. This was getting ridiculous. 'I told you no. I don't have to explain myself.'

'Fine.' Alexa turned back to the case and pulled out a bottle green sundress.

His shoulders slumped with relief. 'Get dressed and I'll call Manuel to have the car ready.'

'Tell him he can drop me at the Castillos' on the way.'

Fury boiled in his blood. 'I told you we're not going.'

She whirled on him, her eyes a stormy grey. 'You told me you weren't going and you didn't explain why. I was invited too, and I'm going. You can either come with me or dine alone. Your choice.'

She stormed into the en suite and slammed the door behind her. The lock clicked and the sound of the shower made him pause. He'd tie her to the bed before he'd join her there. His adopted parents may know him and accept him as he was, but being in their company brought back memories he didn't want to remember, didn't want to have to face all over again. And he didn't want Alexa finding out anything that would make her look at him with disgust.

Alexa wasn't surprised to see Ric perched on the edge of her bed when she returned to her room. His expression was blank, but his eyes held a calculating gleam that made her stomach jitter. She'd calmed down in the shower, although she still couldn't regret her outburst. Why everything about his past had to be a secret, she didn't know, but it boiled her blood that he wouldn't share any part of it with her. Especially after she'd shared a part of herself, and, now, a part of her heart.

Ignoring him, she made her way over to the dressing table, sunk into the chair and reached for her moisturiser. She methodically applied the tinted cream, followed by a light brushing of mascara. Her hair was a swarm of soaked curls and she didn't really want to blow-dry and style it with him watching. It felt too intimate somehow, but he didn't speak or move so she resigned to get on with it.

When her hair was dry, smooth and hanging by her shoulders, he spoke. 'Why don't you leave your hair like that sometimes?'

Alexa looked at her reflection in the mirror. Her face was narrow and flat hair didn't help any. She liked to have it wild, untamed and textured—she thought it suited her personality. But now the messy bed-head do didn't appeal to her like it used to.

Shrugging, she said, 'I will today. I fancy a change.' She painted her lips scarlet, picked up a blotting tissue and smacked her mouth over the material.

'Manuel's picking us up in five minutes.'

She turned to him and frowned. 'I'm going to the barbeque, unless you tell me why you don't want me to.'

He scowled at her and she glared right back, sitting up straight and showing she was unwilling to budge.

'Their home brings back memories I'd rather forget,' he admitted.

She waited a moment, but as expected he gave nothing else away. Giving him a small nod, she reached for her purse and rose from the chair. 'Don't wait up.'

It wasn't like she hadn't known he wouldn't let her go that easily, but it still came as a shock when he reached for her on her way past, wrapped his arms around her waist and had her on her back on the bed so quickly, she wondered if he had superhero powers.

She looked up at him, dazed. 'What the—'

'You said if I explained, you wouldn't go.' His face was rigid with anger, his strong hands pinned her wrists down above her head.

Squirming, she got a leg free and pushed it against his side, trying to move him off. 'You didn't explain, you told me a smidgen of the truth.'

He was way too heavy and her legs still ached from climbing up those bloody stairs, but she kept trying.

'Alexa, stop,' he ordered, his expression blank. Empty. Damn him. She squirmed again. He shifted so his whole body pinned her to the mattress and her breath whooshed out. 'Will you just listen?'

She glowered up at him. The corner of his mouth twitched. 'As you know, Maria and her husband took me off the streets and adopted me.'

She refused to let him off the hook and glared up at him expectantly. His sigh sounded pained.

'Before that I had to do things—horrible things—to survive on the streets.' She felt his body tense above hers and she longed to wrap her arms around him, offer comfort, but he'd pinned them down. 'Maria and Antonio found out about me, what I did, when I stayed briefly with one of their acquaintances. I was fifteen when they took me in and angry at the world. They helped me get on my feet, got me a job and a private tutor and after I'd thrown myself into learning all I could, they gave me the money to take a year out from studying, but I knew they hoped I'd choose to work at the hotel.'

Alexa swallowed against the lump of emotion in her throat. She didn't want to think what he'd had to do to survive—living on the streets was horrific enough and if the haunted look in his

144

eyes was anything to go by, she didn't think she could handle the truth without crying for him, the little boy he'd been. She had a feeling Ric didn't want her tears.

'They haven't let me pay them back.' Anger leaked into his voice and she could tell their gift made him uncomfortable. 'They refuse to take the money I wasted, but I owe so much more than that and more than anything I want them to let me buy into the resort they're building across the city. For them to trust me as a partner. 'I can't stand being there because I don't know what I can do to make it up to them. I can't...I've no idea how to...' He closed his eyes. 'I don't know what they want from me.'

Any defence she had against him crumbled at the pain in his words, in his expression. She lifted her head off the mattress and kissed him hard. Ric's eyes popped open in shock, but he didn't pull away and finally his lids slid shut and he groaned into her mouth. He released his hold on her wrists and she threaded her fingers into his silky hair, caressed his skull.

He pulled back abruptly. She didn't let go of his head, tightened her fingers in his hair. Desire swirled like melted chocolate in his eyes but she could see the fear, the wariness behind it. Her heart thudded.

'They want your love, you idiot, not your money. That's why they want you around, you're their son.'

Ric vaulted off the bed so fast he left her fingers stinging. He glared at her, anger shining from his eyes as he raked a shaky hand through his hair. 'And that's the one thing I can't give them.'

She sat up and glared right back. 'Don't give me that rubbish.' His eyes widened and she knew then she had to knock some sense into his thick skull, was he really so blind he couldn't see how he felt? 'You do love them. Uncomfortable or not, I saw the way you look at Maria and why else would you want to be a part of the business? They're your family, Ric.'

145

He looked at her like she'd grown an extra head. 'You're lecturing me on what I feel? The girl who can't grow up, the girl who runs away from love or marriage, the girl who doesn't even get along with her father?'

She opened her mouth but no words would come. Nothing. He was right. All she did was run away. She'd had a marriage proposal made public by her father in the hope that she'd be embarrassed into accepting it, or whatever his reason. But she knew what love was.

'Just because I don't love him doesn't mean I don't know what love is.' She rose from the bed and stomped over to him. 'I loved my mother, with all my heart. It destroyed me when she died and I blamed him for it.' Ric's face softened, pity shone from his eyes and hers stung with tears. 'You have no idea what I'm capable of. I ran from a proposal because I didn't love the man, didn't even like him. He wasn't who I'd have chosen if marriage was what I wanted.'

'Wanted? So you've changed your mind?' His gaze was filled with disbelief. 'It's a nice lie, Alexa, but it won't work. It won't make me go to the barbeque.'

'Damn the barbeque!' Adrenaline and anger roared through her body. 'It's not a lie. I don't know what I want but I know I can love. I'm not afraid of it like you are.'

'Afraid,' he scoffed. 'I'm not afraid. I don't lie to people. I don't play with their emotions to get what I want.'

'So why are you playing with mine?' she asked.

He focused on her with an intensity that made her wish she could take the question back, for the ground to crack beneath her feet so she could fall into it and be swallowed up, because that question was too close to admitting to him how she felt and right then all she felt was love and anger and helplessness.

'What do you mean?' he asked, all trace of anger gone.

'Nothing. I didn't mean anything by it.' He frowned and she knew he wouldn't let her off that easy. 'Listen, I'm not hungry any more and Manuel will be waiting.' She turned away, hoping he'd just leave but Ric never had done what she wanted him to.

'Alexa, I thought we agreed what this was about. I thought that's what you wanted.'

Sex. She folded her arms and hugged them tight. That was all she wanted, wasn't it? Just because her loopy heart had followed her hormones, didn't mean she wanted Ric forever. A chill ran through her and she shivered. No, she didn't want that. It was hard enough reasoning with him, marriage would be hell.

'That is what we agreed and it's all I want.'

His arms banded around her waist and he nuzzled his nose against her throat. She wanted to lean back into his warmth, wanted the chill inside her to melt, but it wouldn't—not when her emotions were all over the place.

'Then we can get room service, you have to eat.'

His breath tickled her throat and her body sparked to life. Shaking her head, she turned in his arms. 'I'm not hungry. Actually, I'm tired.' Drained and exhausted. 'I'm going to catch up on some sleep.'

He released her, but he didn't leave right away. 'I'll be in the office if you need me.' She nodded. He turned and walked to the door, pausing at the entrance. 'If you feel hungry later, order anything you want,' he said before he shut the door.

Tears welled in her eyes and she blinked them away. She sunk onto the bed, feeling like all the life had been drained out of her. Lying down, she stared at the ceiling and her mind drifted to Ric. His accusation that she had lied felt truer than what she'd said about not fearing love. Because right now she was falling hard and absolutely terrified. Why couldn't she just have kept him at a distance like she managed with everyone else? What was it about

147

this arrogant businessman that had got under her skin?

She slipped into sleep, still not knowing any of the answers.

Another week passed without seeing much of Ric. Alexa knew he needed to be on site more, but his penthouse was so big and quiet without him there. Cold even.

She stacked the huge pile of RSVPs on the table in the kitchen and ticked them off against the names on the guest list. More people than she or Ric were expecting had accepted their invites and the yacht would be at full capacity.

The week had been a blur of organising appointments for Together and hammering out the final details for the party. In the lead up to next Friday, she'd begin decorating the boat since Mark and Justin were back in the States, finalise the flower arrangements and seating plan. There was so much to do, she reckoned enough to keep her occupied and her mind off Ric.

Her phone buzzed and vibrated on the table. She looked at the screen and smiled when she saw Ric's number.

'Hello stranger,' she answered.

His throaty chuckle sent shivers down her spine. 'I'm taking the rest of the night off. Where are you?'

'At home.' Alexa coughed as she realised her folly. 'I mean at *your* home. The penthouse. You know my home's in London. I just meant…well, it's where I'm staying and—'

'Relax, *querida*. I'm on my way there. Are you dressed?'

Her brow furrowed at the excitement in his tone. 'Why would I need to be dressed?'

'I want to take you out, wear something pretty. I'll be there in five minutes.'

'Out where? Wait, Ric—'

'I'm driving, Alexa. I have to go. I've missed you.'

The phone disconnected and she slid it shut, gaped at the device for a second. He *missed* her? He wanted to take her out? Where the hell had grumpy Castillo gone?

Once the shock had cleared, she ran through to her room to find something to wear and then changed her mind. Instead, she ran back to the lift. Removing a sock, she placed it on the floor outside the doors. A few steps later, another sock. Next, she stripped off her blouse and left it hooked on the handle of the door to the hall, all the while excitement coursed through her.

Leaving her thong in the hall and hooking her bra on her bedroom door, she scuttled through to the bed and lay down on the silk in the sexiest pose she could. This, after a week without sex, seemed a better way to make up than going out to some bar or restaurant.

The metal clanking announced the arrival of the lift and her whole body sparked to life. He missed her. And he told her. Her silly heart swelled in her chest. She'd come to realise that her feelings for him were a one way street, and she accepted it, but his confession, however blasé, meant more than she ever thought it would. Still, she didn't have all the answers—like what would happen after the charity ball when she would have to return to London—but she wasn't scared of her love any more. That, at least, felt like progress.

'Alexa,' he called. She waited and heard his laugh. 'I see you still don't follow instructions very well.'

The amusement in his voice sparked the fire in her belly. God, she'd missed him too. He needed to get that gorgeous bum there soon or she'd spontaneously combust.

She readjusted her pose on the bed, just as he swung the door open. The slow smile he treated her to made her heart sputter. His gaze travelled the length of her body, from her head to her toes, lingering on all the nakedness in between.

'So,' she couldn't hide her grin at his obvious arousal. *Welcome*

149

to the club, Ric. 'Where did you want to go?'

'You want to go out, now?' he queried, his gaze trailing over her breasts.

Feeling a bit cheeky, she pinched a nipple between her thumb and forefinger and squeezed. A moan escaped her lips and she swore she heard him growl.

'I want you to get naked and show me just how much you missed me.'

His gaze met hers. 'That can be arranged.'

Slowly, he undid his tie, threw it on the floor. The shirt came next, but he unbuttoned it slowly, only showing a growing slither of hard brown muscle beneath. Her mouth watered and she wanted to get up and rip it off him but she loved that he took his time. It made the anticipation in her tummy build higher.

Finally, he slid the shirt off and went to work on the belt buckle. She could see the growing bulge beneath and wet heat pooled between her thighs. Oh, he was good at this. Without touching her, he'd made her frantic with lust.

Ric stepped out of his black trousers and boxers, his gaze never leaving hers. She licked her lips, her whole body tensed like a predator about to pounce on its prey. When he stalked toward her, she wondered if he felt the same, because he looked like he was about to eat her up.

He walked around to the end her feet hung off and circled her ankles with his palms. 'Ready?' he asked.

'For wh—' but her question was lost in a gasp as he effortlessly pulled her off the bed.

Dropping her ankles, he lifted her up and his mouth crushed hers with an intensity that wasn't far off violence. Alexa kissed him back, digging her fingers into his hair and shoving her tongue into his mouth. She wriggled against him, wanting to be closer, wanting them joined in the most intimate way.

They fell onto the bed, twisting so she landed on his chest. She broke the kiss and gasped in a lungful of air. Her body felt like it had been deprived of this for so long, she couldn't wait. Straddling his hips, she slid over the solid length of him, feeling his rapid pulse against her centre.

His lips found her breasts and he nibbled the swollen skin, sucked each nipple and caressed her bum. She rose, grabbed the base of his erection and heard his sharp intake of breath before she lowered herself on the length of him.

'Alexa, *querida*.'

His voice sounded like he was in pain and she almost was. Stretched to the point she wondered if she'd split in two, she froze. His thumb found her swollen nub and he rubbed it with enough pressure to send little jolts of pleasure coursing through her.

'You're not ready,' he said with his jaw taut, eyes half-crazed.

She smiled down at him. 'I can't wait.'

She rose until just the tip of him was inside her, and then sank down. This time her body opened and she took as much of him as she could. His ragged breathing drowned out her moan of bliss, his thumb on her encouraged the pressure to build and swirl. Holding his shoulders she rode him hard, digging her nails into his flesh and drawing a ragged groan from his throat.

He watched her through hooded eyes, his expression softened by arousal, his hips pumped up to meet each of her thrusts and she couldn't take her gaze off his face. A sense of power stole through her as her orgasm built deep inside. She slammed down on him harder, faster. The scent of sweat and their lovemaking filled her senses and her heart burst open as an orgasm shuddered to her core.

She detonated like a crate of dynamite, but refused to collapse and fall like she wanted to. Instead she rode him through the waves until his thigh muscles went rigid, his jaw stiffened and he grabbed both her hips and pumped up and into her like a mad man. The pressure and heat twisted, built and released all over again and she convulsed, shuddered and fell onto his sweat soaked chest.

Ric thrust up one last time, lodging himself deep as he trembled through his own orgasm. Using the last ounce of her strength, she squeezed her internal muscles, drawing a groan and the last of his pleasure from him.

His arms wrapped around her waist, held her so tight she struggled to breathe but she didn't care. In that moment, she wanted him to pull her inside him, so she'd never have to leave. There, she'd finally admitted it to herself and the world hadn't swallowed her up. She wanted to stay with Ric, there in his arms, and never let go.

Chapter Twelve

'I need a shower,' Alexa grumbled.

She sat up on the bed, taking her body heat with her. Ric grabbed her around the waist and dragged her back to his side, pleased with her lack of protest. 'Later,' he whispered against her sweat-damp hair.

Snuggling into his chest, she let out a contented sigh. His arms tightened around her. All week, he'd missed her so much that his mind constantly drifted from the boring meetings, the deal and instead focused on Alexa. Leaving at dawn and returning well after sunset should have tired him out, but the truth was he had been full of restless energy. The pull in his chest had become increasingly painful. He thought having her in his arms, sated and sleepy, would ease the feeling. After an afternoon of spectacular sex, it only seemed to intensify.

Ric was beginning to think a measly week with her wouldn't be enough. His chest tightened and he hugged her closer, panic racing his heart. It would have to be enough. She was leaving for London. His life and routine would return. A few weeks ago, that would have made him happy. But now...

Now his old life looked empty. There was no fun, no joy, no Alexa.

She lifted her head off his chest and smiled at him. With her

153

eyes half-mast and her hair wild and mussed, he thought she looked more beautiful than he'd ever seen her. His heart squeezed in his chest.

'How did it go?' she asked.

Ric knew she meant the building work, but he couldn't resist teasing her. 'On a scale of one to ten, I think your performance gets an eleven.'

She grinned and smacked his chest. 'I meant at the site, wise guy.'

He grabbed a lock of her soft, silky hair and twirled it around his finger. 'The new design and build contract is signed. In a month, six weeks at most, the complex should be ready for the designers.'

'I'm glad it went okay.' She kissed his chest.

'How has your week been?'

The feel of her lips on his chest had his tired body wanting things it should know it wasn't in any state for.

'Good. I have all the details for the party hammered down. And I got a few more clients for Together.'

He stroked her hair as she continued to plant butterfly kisses on his chest. Goosebumps rose on his skin.

'What kind of business do you have?' The fact he still didn't know made him feel like a selfish bastard. It wasn't that he hadn't asked her, but every time something else had come up.

Her lips began a torturous trail down his abs. 'I match up travelling business men and women who don't want to dine or sightsee alone with people with similar interests.' Her teeth nipped his hips and he gasped. 'It's quite popular.'

Confusion shot through the lust in his mind. 'And these people who dine or sightsee with the business men and woman, who are they?'

'Students mostly.' She licked the head of his erection and sucked the tip into her mouth. His hands fisted on the silk sheets. 'People who are available at a moment's notice.'

154

In other words, people who needed money so badly they'd do anything to make a quick euro. People who would reject their pride and self-respect in order to survive. People like him, who'd been trapped at the bottom looking desperately for shelter, food and a way to live through another day. His whole body ran cold and stiffened, except the part she coaxed with her tongue.

'Ric, what's wrong?' Those eyes, seemingly innocent and kind, turned his stomach. He rose from the bed. 'Where are you going?'

He pulled on a pair of briefs, then his suit trousers. Just as he'd shrugged into his shirt, she was in front of him, hurt clear in every line of her face. But he didn't feel guilt, he felt numb.

'Talk to me.' She reached out a hand but he backed away.

'Don't touch me.'

Her mouth dropped open. 'What did I say?'

Her voice cracked and for a second the pull toward her intensified until he thought the force of it would bring her close, but he ignored it. He closed his eyes, focused on every shred of emotion and forced it down into the dark recesses of his being. It was a skill he'd learned years ago, a skill that kept him strong.

'I think a room has become available. I'll arrange to have your luggage taken there.' Yesterday the receptionist had informed him a room was free, but he hadn't known then what kind of person he'd invited into his home.

'I don't understand why you're acting like this.' She blocked the door, defiance etched on her face and something he refused to acknowledge shone from her eyes.

'I'd rather not have the owner of an *escort* company in my home.'

Her eyes grew wide. 'Together isn't a bloody escort company!'

'No, it's a classier version disguised as something innocent, but you sell people to others to make a living. Women like you disgust me.'

Ric ignored the tears glittering in her eyes and shoved passed her into the hall. He stalked to the lounge and buzzed down to reception. Once he'd given orders to have Alexa's things moved to another room, he turned to find her watching him. She'd dressed in a silk robe that fell down to her knees. She hugged the pale pink material tight to her body.

'It's not what you think, Ric. I don't set people up for sex, just company. I'd sack anyone who did otherwise.' Her eyes pleaded with him but he didn't feel a thing. Didn't allow himself to. 'I'll move but I don't want this to be the end.'

He forced a harsh laugh through the lump in his throat. 'What do you want Alexa?' He stalked toward her, pulled his face into his hardest expression. 'Marriage, kids, forever with a man like me?' She swallowed, and he went on, ignoring every instinct inside him screaming to shut his mouth. 'A man who grew up on the streets? A man who was forced to sell his body for a warm place to stay for the night? I'm sure the great Robert Green would welcome me to the family with open arms.'

Tears welled in her eyes and spilled over. His heart squeezed again, but he refused to acknowledge it. She should know how tainted he was. Maybe then when he threw her out, he wouldn't feel the guilt.

'Ric, I—'

'Save your pity for someone who deserves it. I want you to pack your things and leave.' She stepped back, away from the fury pounding out from him. 'What you're running is sick, the kind of thing that destroys people and you don't care as long as you have money for a new pair of skyscraper heels.'

She wiped her face with her hands, but more tears fell. 'That's not what I do.'

'I expect you to stay away until you leave and I don't want to see you at the ball on Friday.'

He saw the pain replace itself with anger in her eyes. 'Are you kidding? After all I've done—'

'I do not want the charity to be tainted by the reputation of someone who earns money by destroying people.'

'You know, you are an arse. An arrogant, pushy, thick-skulled, arse.' She stormed through to her room then emerged a few minutes later with the suitcases and holdall. The realisation she hadn't yet unpacked hit him like a blow. 'You can't see the truth about anything because you're so scared to open up. I get that, I was there too. But to accuse me of this is a step too far. You know me. You know I wouldn't hurt anyone.'

'I knew the act you put on, the woman who agreed to do this to help herself, her reputation and her illicit business.'

She stared at him hard but not with disgust or pity, it was disappointment. His stomach clenched. The elevator doors opened and a bellboy came in. Alexa handed over her luggage and followed the man to the door. She turned back to him, pain so clear on her face that it knocked the breath out of him.

'That's why I did all this to begin with. But when I went to Santos grovelling, and when I called in a favour to my father, it wasn't me I was thinking about.' She stepped into the elevator and the doors slid shut behind her.

Ric stalked through to the kitchen, telling himself that it was a lie. No one could be a good person and run an escort agency, no matter how they tried to dress it up. He hadn't been part of an agency, his clients had come from word of mouth, from suggestive comments he'd made to women on the street. The thought almost made him double over with nausea.

But he'd changed. He'd shoved all the memories down and was trying to become a better person. A man who worked hard for the people who saved him. He paused in front of the fridge, a picture of himself and Alexa shooting out of one of the tube slides at Water World stuck there. His face looked young, like a twenty-eight year olds should, and Alexa looked happier than he'd ever seen her.

Her pale, tear soaked face before she left was a sharp contrast, and he'd done that. He couldn't fight the guilt. But he had dedicated his free time to help vulnerable children and Alexa made money from selling people like that. People like he had been.

He opened the fringe and pulled out a bottle of wine, unscrewed the lid and brought it to his lips. None of it mattered. She was out of his life now and it could return to the way it was supposed to be, with him paying for his past by helping others and not enjoying life.

Friday arrived and Alexa couldn't stand the confines of her tiny room any more. She kicked at the sand with her flip flops as she sauntered along the beach, watching the tourists sunbathe, play football and splash around in the sea. It seemed everywhere she looked people were happy.

He had ripped her heart out, stomped on it, and then handed it to her on a skewer. She'd been so terrified of falling for someone who would rule her life, she hadn't considered the ramifications of being rejected.

How could he think she'd pimp people out? Every time she'd thought of his past, of his confession, tears welled in her eyes and a lump lodged in her throat. She could understand why he might assume that at first, but he *knew* her. How could he think she'd run an escort company after all the time they had spent together?

She didn't know any of the answers by the time she reached a fenced off part of the beach. Looking up, she saw the Castillos' boathouse and her heart skipped a few beats. Turning, she started to hurry away when Maria called her name.

'Alexa. What are you doing here?'

She turned back to see Maria walking towards the fence in an elegant sundress. After popping the lock and swinging the gate open, she stepped aside to let Alexa past.

'I was out for a walk, I didn't mean to intrude.'

'You're not intruding, sweetheart. I've been meaning to call you.'

Alexa turned to her. 'Why?'

'Take a seat.' She gestured to a chair and Alexa slid onto it. 'Can I get you something to drink?'

'Water would be lovely.'

Maria waved at a man shuffling furniture about and fired instructions at him in Spanish. Alexa guessed that's where Ric got his domineering side from. Maria sat down next to Alexa and turned to her, a serious expression on her face. 'What happened with you and Enrique?'

Tears welled in her eyes at the mention of his name and she had to choke back a sob. 'Nothing. We're...not seeing each other.'

Maria grabbed her hand and ran her thumb over the back. Alexa felt some warmth seep into her skin from the touch, but her insides still felt icy cold.

'But he loves you.'

Alexa couldn't fight the tears this time, they poured from her eyes like water from a tap. 'He...I...he doesn't know what love is.'

She was wrapped in Maria's embrace before she knew what happened. Her sobs turned into soft sniffles as the older woman rubbed her back. The expensive perfume and motherly touch reminded Alexa of the comfort she'd felt when her own mother hugged her. When she relaxed enough to stop crying, Maria released her.

'Sweetheart, he doesn't think he deserves love. He never has, but I know he loves you. He's been miserable all week.'

'He was here?' she asked, wondering if they were talking about the same man. He hadn't looked miserable when he'd horsed her out.

159

'He's been here every night. Alexa, I don't know what happened between the two of you, but he was happy. You've gotten him to open up to us, and my husband and I are forever in your debt. Can't the two of you work things out?'

'He thinks I'm a pimp,' she blurted. Tears welled up in her eyes again and by the shock on Maria's face, Alexa wished she had better control over what popped out of her mouth.

'My business, Together, he thinks it's an escort agency, but it's not.'

Understanding softened her gaze, but her eyes were wary. 'I know, a few of my friends have used the company when they've been in London. It's a brilliant idea. Most people in our circles hate to dine alone, but when they're away on business they don't have much of a choice.'

'But because of his past, he can't see that,' she said, remembering Ric had told her the Castillos knew everything. 'He thinks I'm using vulnerable people to make money by selling them.'

She frowned, irritation warring with love in her expression. 'Let me talk to him. I'll make him see sense.'

The man brought the drink and placed it on the table in front of them. She watched as the sun shone on the glass and reflected white light onto Maria's diamond engagement ring. What was the point in getting through to him? What was the point in changing his mind when she'd be leaving for London in a few days anyway?

Ric wouldn't marry her. He didn't think he was good enough for her. Her father would approve, despite what Ric thought, but could she up and leave her best friends? Her business? Her life? For a man who didn't even know what love meant.

'Don't worry about it Mrs Castillo. Things happen for a reason.' She rose, telling herself that this happened to make her stronger. She'd bounce back and be okay. Eventually. 'Thank you for being so kind.'

'Alexa, I want you to come to the ball tonight.'

She couldn't agree. 'Ric said I wasn't allowed.'

From the look on Maria's face, she'd like to show Ric who wasn't allowed. 'Just be ready, I'll make sure he changes his mind.'

She smiled and said goodbye without promising anything. Ric wouldn't change his mind. He didn't know the concept of compromise. As she made her way back to the hotel, hope swelled in her tummy and she didn't bat it back down. Didn't want to. Maybe this time when he let her down her silly heart would realise he wasn't worth loving.

Everything was going to hell. The wrong amount of flowers had been delivered and the deck of the yacht was bursting with them; there weren't enough centrepieces for the tables and the buffet list Alexa had given his chef had gone missing. Add that to the clawing despair in his stomach and Ric swore this was the worst day of his life.

He barked orders to the waiters, asking them to return to the hotel to find whatever centrepieces they could from storage, ordered the maids to dispose of a fifth of the flowers and cursed himself for telling Alexa she couldn't come. He needed her help.

'Do you have a minute?' A familiar voice asked.

He turned to see Maria, her arms folded across her chest and a stern expression on her face. His stomach dropped. She hadn't looked at him like that since he announced he was going to race speedboats. 'I'm busy at the moment.'

'You wouldn't be run off your feet if you hadn't sacked the best thing that's ever happened to you.' Anger leaked into her voice. He'd never heard her speak that way.

'It's better if Alexa isn't here.' But the words tasted sour and didn't ring true, even to his own ears.

Maria crossed the distance between them, pulled a small leaflet out of her bag and handed it to him. He frowned at her.

'No, it isn't darling. Read that. And you might want to talk to the Martinas, the Carreros and a few others who regularly visit London for business. You'll see that you have an apology to make.'

He looked down at the leaflet, a guide to the best hotels in London. Opening it, he saw the advertisement on the inside cover. *'Together, matching your intellect and interests for your time in London.'*

Intellect and Interests? Ric huffed out a disbelieving laugh.

'It's not an escort company. The small print states that they match people with similar interests to keep the client company while they're alone on business. I know a few women and men who've hired Alexa for this. Ric, do you honestly think Robert Green would allow this to go on in The Crystal if it were anything else? Do you really believe Alexa would do that?'

He swallowed. Deep down he knew she wouldn't. He'd spent the better part of the night before looking over reviews and researching the company, all the while knowing he wouldn't find anything untoward. But what did it matter? He would struggle through tonight alone and manage. He always did. Alexa was leaving in a few days and his apology would be for what? A couple of days in bed? He wouldn't do that to her. Couldn't. It would be using her like they'd both been used in the past.

'Ric, talk to her. Let her help you tonight.'

He looked into the eyes of the woman who'd become his mother and his chest swelled with an emotion so strong, so all consuming that he knew Alexa had been right. He did love Maria and her husband. He'd just been too scared to acknowledge it before.

'There's no reason why she would help me.' What he said to her on Monday couldn't be taken back easily.

'She will help you because she loves you.'

He blinked. 'She doesn't love me. If anything, she'll help so she

162

can take the credit.'

The words burned his tongue on the way out. He knew they were a lie and he felt foolish for saying them. Her parting words rang in his head. Why had she helped? Had she done it for him?

'Enrique Castillo you're a stubborn, foolish man if you believe that.' There it was again, the anger. He knew he deserved it.

'I don't, not really.'

Her lips curved and warmth filled her eyes. 'Then what are you waiting for?'

Alexa opened the door and her eyes grew wide. Ric couldn't take his gaze off her. Dark smudges beneath the silvery orbs broke his heart. The pullover he'd stripped from her body weeks ago seemed to hang on her tiny frame and her usually messy hair was sleek and straight, skimming past her shoulder blades. His heart almost burst out of his chest.

'What do you want, Ric?' she asked with false bravado.

'You.' It was the only truthful answer.

He grabbed her waist, hauled her against him and his mouth found hers with an urgency he didn't know was there until he saw her. She kissed him back, threaded her fingers into his hair and pulled him closer. Picking her up, he walked them into the room and kicked the door shut behind him. Lust heated his blood. The warmth and emotion bursting out of him now doubled the love he felt for Maria.

Alexa froze in his arms and ripped her mouth from his. The pain in her eyes broke his heart, and when she pulled away she took half of it with her.

'No.' Her voice shook. '*No.*'

'I didn't mean...' He cleared his throat. 'I came here to apologise, not to kiss you.' The look she gave him was full of disbelief. 'I know your business isn't what I initially assumed. I'm sorry,

163

Alexa. I should never have doubted you.'

She stood frozen and silent. He longed to pull her back into his arms, but knew he'd risk pushing her too hard, too fast. 'I want you to finish what you came here to, and then I want you to come to the ball with me. As my date.'

Anger sparked the storm in her eyes. 'You want my help? That's what this is about? Go bugger yourself Ric.' She stormed past him and pulled the door open. 'Get out.'

'Yes, I want your help, but I want you with me too.'

'Why?'

He sucked in a deep breath, knowing that once he said the words he would be more vulnerable than he had ever been living on the streets. Sharing love with two people he knew loved him was one thing; putting his heart on the line to be rejected was another. But he was sick of running scared. Sick of chasing anything to fill the void inside him when the answer stood in front of him. He needed Alexa in his life. Needed the light and fun and carefree spirit that she brought.

'I love you and I don't care what happens next. I don't care what the media find. I want you, and only you. I can live through the rest.'

Her mouth fell open and silent tears streamed down her face. 'What if they dig up your past, like you're scared they will? What if one of those women sells their story? What about your reputation?'

'It's terrifying, Alexa. I've hidden from my past for so long, to have it made public used to be my biggest fear, but it's not any more.' The tears continued to stream down her face and his thumb itched to wipe them away, but he wasn't sure she'd let him. 'Losing you scares me more than anything else.'

'I…I don't know what to say,' she whispered.

Ric almost laughed. Almost. If his heart hadn't been smashed into a million shards he would have found the humour her statement should have brought. Alexa always knew what she wanted to say.

'Tell me what you want and you can have it,' he said.

She frowned at him, despite the tears. 'Like I could go anywhere I wanted to for dinner?'

'No. I mean anything. If you want me, I'm yours. If you want marriage, I'll have you down the aisle so fast you won't be able to change your mind. If you want me to leave you alone...' He swallowed hard. 'I...I can do that too.'

Her body trembled and his froze, waiting for her answer.

'I need time to think. I can't just decide now.'

He nodded, fought the urge to demand to know now. After all he had done, he could wait for her.

'I'll get dressed and help you with the prep. Is everything okay with the flowers?'

Ric shook his head. 'Too many flowers, not enough centrepieces, the chef has lost the menu and I haven't had a chance to check the seating plan.'

She shook her head and smiled. 'I'll fix it. Promise.'

He believed her like he should have done last week. Before he left, he turned around. 'Whatever you want, it's yours.' He trailed a path down her damp cheek with his finger. 'I mean it, Alexa. I love you.'

She looked up at him, her eyes open, wide, terrified. 'I believe you.'

He closed the door, knowing there was nothing else he could do. He'd laid his soul bare and given her all the control against his nature. Now all he had to do was pray Maria was right. Pray Alexa loved him enough not to run away.

After dealing with the flowers, finding more centrepieces, rewriting the menu from memory and adding a few table places for guests that hadn't RSVP'd, Alexa felt like superwoman.

For the last hour, she'd introduced her father to everyone she had met when she was out with Ric, except for him. She still hadn't made a decision and it wouldn't be fair to him to bestow Robert upon him.

Now, Robert was chatting to Santos sans his she-devil wife—some nonsense about the state of economies and the benefits of joining the Euro. Her gaze wandered over the guests mingling, snatching themselves a pitiful portion of food from the buffet, and then across to the rail. Taking her chances swimming to shore was more tempting than the chocolate fudge cake she'd insisted be served.

'Would you like to dance?' Ric's whisper in her ear made goose-bumps rise on her skin.

Her heart throbbed out an unhealthy beat which made her wonder again about the heart attack. When she turned to see him in a tux, his expression so open and pain clear in his eyes, she quickly changed her mind. Her heart was broken, not unhealthy.

'Yes.'

The smile he gave her brightened his whole face and her belly flipped.

'Alexa, I don't believe you have introduced us.'

Damn. Her heart raced as Robert turned from his conversation with Santos who excused himself. 'Father, this is Enrique Castillo. He's the founder of this charity event.'

Ric extended his hand to her father. 'Alexa did most of the work.'

'Really?' Robert's incredulous tone grated on her nerves.

Ric nodded seriously and she thought she saw a hint of anger burn in his eyes. Her father turned to her and really *looked* at her. Everything inside squirmed and wriggled under his scrutiny. He sent her one of his genuine smiles which crinkled his eyes and made her heart throb. When he smiled at her like that she wondered if that's why her mother fell in love with him in the first place.

'Alexa, I am very impressed.'

She blinked, and her lips parted. It was the first time he had told her that.

Ric's arm slid around her waist and he stepped in close to her side. Her heart pounded wildly in her chest. 'Your daughter is an amazing woman, Mr Green. I couldn't have organised the event without her.'

Robert assessed Ric for a second, then gave another of his smiles. 'Did I hear you ask my daughter to dance?' At Ric's nod, he continued. 'Then don't let me keep you. I'm sure there will be lots of time to get to know one another.'

After another handshake, her father left them. She gaped at his retreating back, wondering what the imposter had done with her father. Then again, maybe now that she was acting with a little more class, Robert was beginning to see her for the young woman she was, not the terrible teenager who'd caused him so much grief. Hope swelled when she considered that things might even get better between them.

Ric traced a finger from the cut in her dress up her spine, drawing her back to reality. Her skin tingled all over at the touch. Alexa turned to him and smiled. 'Thank you.'

'How about that dance?'

She followed him onto the dance floor amongst the other couples swaying to the light jazz band. There was so many emotions jittering around inside, Alexa couldn't think about anything at all. All she knew was that being without Ric was killing her spirit, but there were still too many barriers in the way. Even a quick call to Sarah and Jenna didn't solve anything, but when Sarah mentioned a double wedding next year, Alexa didn't feel the usual chill which usually accompanied thoughts of marriage.

Ric pulled her close and she slid her hands onto his shoulders.

Looking up into his eyes, misery seeped from her pores at the desperate hope on his face. She guessed he wasn't scared of showing his emotions any more, least of all to her.

Darting a glance around the room, she spotted a few specifically chosen reporters and photographers. She couldn't doubt that he didn't care about their relationship going public, because the whole world would know if she decided to be with him.

'Alexa, the waiting is painful.'

She snapped her attention back to him. Her heart bounced into her throat at the look in his eyes. They swayed with the gentle rhythm of the boat and turned to the music. She couldn't keep the reasons for not being together inside any more.

'We argue all the time,' she blurted. His eyebrows rose, but he continued to lead her. 'You refuse to compromise. I don't want to be a possession. I don't want to be your woman at home waiting up all night for you to finish work. If I stay, I'll be lonely.'

'We haven't argued much lately.' His slow grin jellified her knees. 'Before, I wanted to hide my past from you. I didn't want you to look at me with disgust. I should have known you wouldn't, Alexa, but I was scared. I didn't want you to get close so I pushed you away, I ordered you around because I like control. I can work on loosening up.'

The grin slipped from his face. 'Maria and Antonio have asked if I want to buy into the new resort and the hotel. I can't do all that myself and they're both hoping to be silent partners so I've been interviewing for an area manager, someone who can deal with all the urgent matters so I won't have to.

'Before you came here my life was dull. You showed me how to live and I don't want to go back to the boring me.'

Tears welled and streamed down her face. His thumb rubbed them away. 'What if I can't keep my mouth shut next time stick-insect or someone like her insults me? With my reputation, you'll lose all the respect you worked hard for. You could lose everyone here.'

Determination flared in his eyes and hardened his jaw. He slid a hand up her back and twined his fingers in the hair at her nape. Her breath and heartbeats sped when she realised what he planned to do. Before she could think, his lips crashed down on hers and she was lost in him. The party melted away as she pressed her whole body against him, linked her hands behind his head and parted her lips.

He plundered her mouth in a sensual torture that made a slow-burn flush through her veins. When he pulled away she opened her eyes to the flash of cameras pointed at them. Panic stole through her as she darted her head around.

'Alexa, I don't care about what anyone else thinks. Just you. And if anyone else treats you like Mrs Santos did, I'll deal with it.' He leaned in closer and whispered, 'If you love me, I don't need anything else, but what do you want?' He pulled her back into the dance, ignoring the prying eyes and flashing bulbs from the cameras.

'I want you to tell me the truth.' She looked up at him. 'Tell me how you got the scar. Tell me what the nightmare was about.'

His whole body stiffened as she waited for his answers. Panic pitched in her tummy again. She'd started to believe they could work, but if he couldn't share himself with her, how could they be together?

He controlled whatever emotions he felt and leaned back in to whisper, 'I was stabbed when I was fifteen by another home-less man who wanted my spot for shelter. The nightmares—' His breath caught and she pulled back to study his face.

The haunted look in his eyes melted her heart. 'You don't have to tell me.'

'I'll tell you everything you want to know. They're all from my time living on the streets. Sometimes it feels like I'm back there.'

More tears spilled down her face as her soul hurt for the little boy he'd been, afraid and alone.

'Don't cry for me, *querida*.' His thumbs brushed the tears away. 'I'm happy now. Have been since you stumbled into my home in your undergarments.'

Alexa laughed, the tears clogged her throat and made her sputter a little. 'And the extreme sports?'

Ric frowned, like he was thinking how to answer. 'I felt empty for a long time. I think I wanted to feel alive, but now I know adrenaline wasn't what I was looking for.' He bumped his nose against hers.

'Where would we live?' It was the last hurdle for her. Could she up and leave her life?

After he spun her around again, he answered, 'Wherever you want. London, here, India, I don't care as long as I'm with you.'

She rose on her tiptoes and kissed him, briefly this time thinking she'd given the press enough to write about for a while. 'I love you.'

'And I love you.' His arms banded around her waist. 'We'll work out everything else together.'

Epilogue

'Lex if you don't come up here I swear on Dior I'll hurt you.'

Alexa scurried to her feet. When Jenna swore on Dior, she was serious and if her scowl was anything to go by, her patience was at an end. Smoothing down the pink silk bridesmaid dress, Alexa turned back to plead Ric with her eyes.

The smug git grinned. 'I'm not helping you out of this one, Green. You're on your own.'

She pouted and his smile grew wider. 'So much for giving me everything I want.'

Just then Jenna grabbed her hand and hauled her into the crowd of squirming women who were trying to push their way to the front of the herd. Alexa decided if she stayed at the back of the crazy women, her feet wouldn't get crippled. Jenna threw herself among the thrall and Alexa giggled. She'd never seen anyone so keen on catching a bouquet, especially considering Jenna was next in line to get married.

Sarah climbed onto a chair with her husband hiking up the skirts of her stunning, handmade gown. She reminded Alexa of Snow White or some other fairy-tale princess. Happiness swelled in her heart as she watched the exchange between Sarah and her new husband, giggling and kissing, they looked head-over-heels in love. Exactly how she felt when she was with Ric. Well, when he wasn't letting her mad-hatter friends push her into doing this.

Sarah held the bouquet up for all to see. White tulips entwined in red ribbons fluttered in the April breeze. Goosebumps rose on her skin and she rubbed her bare arms, wishing she was back in Marbella. She'd forgotten how cold London could be in the spring.

'Right, ladies. On the count of three.' Sarah turned her back to the crowd of women.

They went bonkers, pushing one another, jumping and standing on the tip toes of their skyscraper heels to gain a measly inch in the hope of catching the bloody thing. Alexa grinned when she saw Jenna squirming among the others.

Sarah began a painfully slow countdown and she turned to look for Ric. He wore a smug grin and had a dark look in his eye that made her tummy flip. The git knew she didn't want to be involved in this part of the ceremony. If she was going to get married, it would be because he proposed to her, not because she caught a bunch of flowers and guilted him into it.

'Three!'

Alexa turned back to the screaming crowd just in time to see a blur of red and white flash in front of her eyes. The bouquet smacked her off the cheek and she stumbled back, her hands flying to her stinging face.

'Alexa!' Sarah shouted over the crowd of woman diving to the floor to get the bouquet.

Warm hands turned her around and she looked up into dark eyes shining with concern. '*Querida*, are you okay?'

She grinned up at Ric and slid her hands around his neck. 'Mortified, but okay.'

He closed the distance between their heads and pressed his lips to hers. Her skin prickled, but she didn't think it had anything to do with the bouquet hitting her face. Standing on her tiptoes, she pressed herself closer. Ric pulled away and she whimpered.

Chuckling, he turned to look at Sarah and winked. Alexa frowned up at him. 'What was that about?'

'I didn't think her aim would be that good.'

She gasped. 'You told Sarah to throw the bouquet at me?'

Grinning down at her, he said, 'Of course. How else was I going to persuade you to marry me? You were supposed to catch it though, not let it knock you out.'

Her jaw dropped as she stared at him, unable to believe he'd gone to so much trouble. What happened to getting down on one knee with a ring?

A frown formed between his brows and she held her breath, waiting for the rest. 'I spoke with your father today when you were helping Sarah get ready.'

A swarm of butterflies invaded her tummy. 'What about?'

He darted a glance around the gazebo. Hundreds of guests had attended the wedding and Alexa was glad Sarah's grandfather's country manor was big enough to hold them all.

'Come.'

Ric escorted her away from the ruckus to the edge of the tent. He slid into a chair at an empty table and pulled her onto his lap. 'Since you two are building a relationship, I wanted to be honest with him.'

Again, Alexa was shocked speechless. In the six months since her father had come to the charity ball in Marbella, Ric hadn't mentioned that he wanted to get to know Robert or share the dark secrets of his past with him—even though he'd told her almost everything. It hurt her so much even though she knew he kept the worst of his memories from her.

She wished she had a time machine so she could go back and save the terrified little boy who was abandoned by his mother. But for him to tell Robert too, since the press hadn't dug very deep, Alexa realised that he truly did mean what he said. He wasn't afraid of losing respect any more. All he cared about losing was her.

So far she'd worked through a lot of her issues with her father, and apologies had been made on both sides. After all these years, she didn't know how she managed to keep a grudge when she could have had her father through it all.

Ric snared her hands in his. 'Alexa, you're it for me. You're my whole life. I had to tell Robert everything and prove to him that I still deserve you. I don't want to lose you.'

Her throat felt thick. 'You'd never lose me,' she whispered. Pulling a hand free, she reached up and stroked his smooth jaw. 'What did he say?'

'He said he respected me for letting him know, but it didn't change his opinion of me. And when I asked for your hand in marriage he gave us his blessing.'

Tears welled up and spilled over so quickly she didn't have a chance to wipe them away. He placed a hand on either side of her head and wiped the moisture with his thumbs. Her heart worked overtime and her chest swelled at the love and adoration in his eyes. When he looked at her like that, she felt like the centre of his universe.

One corner of his mouth tilted. 'So, Green, what do you say? Do you want to be my wife?'

Alexa loved this man with all her heart, but she couldn't resist a little payback. After all, the sneak freak planned to trick her into marriage. 'I'll marry you.' The pride and love in his expression took her breath away, but she forced herself to drag in a breath. 'On one condition.'

He stared her down and she could see the confusion in his wary gaze. 'What's the condition?'

'We do one last wild thing before we become boring old farts.'

Ric's whole body shook as he laughed. 'What did you have in mind?'

'I want to bungee jump out of a helicopter with you.'

His face paled a shade and Alexa smirked. 'Not man enough any more, Castillo?'

He slid his arms around her waist and hauled her closer on his lap. 'I'm man enough for any of your crazy ideas, Green.'

And he spent the rest of his life proving to her that he was.

Printed by RR Donnelley at Glasgow, UK